INCIDENT AT BADAMYÂ

DOROTHY GILMAN

Incident
at Badamyâ

Doubleday
NEW YORK LONDON TORONTO SYDNEY AUCKLAND

Published by Doubleday, a division of
Bantam Doubleday Dell Publishing Group, Inc.
666 Fifth Avenue, New York, New York 10103

Doubleday and the portrayal of an anchor
with a dolphin are trademarks of Doubleday,
a division of Bantam Doubleday Dell Publishing Group, Inc.

Library of Congress Cataloging-in-Publication Data
Gilman, Dorothy, 1923–
    Incident at Badamyâ/Dorothy Gilman.—1st ed.
      p.   cm.
    I. Title.
PS3557.I433I54   1989
813'.54—dc19   88-16171
                                           CIP

ISBN: 0-385-24760-5
Copyright © 1989 by Dorothy Gilman Butters
All Rights Reserved
Printed in the United States of America
April 1989
First Edition
BG

PROLOGUE

IN THE SOHO DISTRICT of New York there is a small marionette theater inserted between two warehouse lofts, a theater that has known fame twice, first in the mid-sixties when it was discovered by theater critics, given reviews in *Newsweek* and *Time* and a cover story in *Life* magazine, and again in the late seventies when the theater produced an authentic Burmese production of the Creation of the World, with the twenty-drum *saing waing* and gongs, cymbals, songs and puppet dances, followed by a tale from the Jataka.

The creator of this theater, and its puppetmaster, is a radiant little woman who frequently wears a colorful *longyi* but is not Burmese. Occasionally she is interviewed but says very little about her personal life or her past, preferring to speak of the long great history of the *yokthe pwe*—the puppet theater—in Burma. There is known to be a husband and two young children, a boy named Sein and a girl called Mi-Mi. Only once in being interviewed has she been asked precisely when she left Burma, and this by a New York *Times* feature writer who had spent months there during the war with Merrill's Marauders and knew the country well. Appalled, he said, "But that was a hellish year in Upper Burma, surely you had enormous trouble in leaving?"

He was surprised by the curious little smile that curved her lips. Her glance moved past him to a marionette prominently displayed on the wall, an exquisitely carved little puppet dressed in a flame-red costume and carrying a crimson wand in one hand. She said softly, "Only at Badamyâ," and adroitly changed the subject by offering him a cup of tea.

INCIDENT AT BADAMYÂ

1

THERE HAD BEEN OMENS.

Mr. San Ya, drawing his horoscopes by the light of a candle, had seen at once that the new month was not auspicious; he had painstakingly drawn it a second time but still it promised only more violence . . . his country was experiencing a difficult birth. The Prime Minister had announced there would be peace in one year but that announcement had been issued two years ago and the rail line to Rangoon was still cut, the roads unsafe, and the insurgents split into even newer fragments. What was one to make of them all: the AFPFL of the government, the Red Flag Communists, the White Flag Communists, the PVO divided into White Banner and Yellow Banner factions, the KNDO, and lately the battles fought against the KMT who sought sanctuary in the north from Mao in China?

Most ominous of all were the bandits, the *dacoits,* who had leaped into the vacuum.

Mr. San Ya sighed as he blew out his candle and retired to the mat on the floor with his sleeping family. He was not a man given to worry but in those moments before sleep seized him he had lately begun pondering how his small village on the Irrawaddy might acquire another gun. There was only one gun in the village, tonight in the hands of Ba Pe, whose turn it was to stand guard until dawn, but one was not enough. As usual Mr. San Ya's thoughts wandered to the foreigner in their midst and he considered again how he might tactfully inquire of Mr. Ferris if he owned a gun. It was Mr. San Ya's opinion, somewhat prejudiced, that a foreigner with a sixteen-year-old daughter to protect had a duty to own a gun even if the man was a Christian and had been a missionary before his *leikpya*—his soul—had sickened. Like the Prime Minister, Mr. Ferris had announced many months ago that the "tumult and the shouting," as he phrased it, would soon go away and that he intended to "brave the storm"—he spoke like that—but in the vocabulary of the British under whom Mr. San Ya had once served he thought him a bloody fool: he had stayed too long. He thought that Mr. Ferris would have been surprised to learn that he was regarded with kindly tolerance strictly because of his daughter Gen, who Ma Nu insisted was protected by a *thamma deva.* That she was protected by a thamma deva was quite possible, thought Mr. San Ya, nodding judiciously, but if that was the case then Mr. Ferris would not need a gun and might be persuaded to lend it to the village. If, of course, he possessed one.

Persistent worry was not in Mr. San Ya's nature and presently his eyes closed and a snore escaped him. Outside, the full moon poured its milky light over the village, bleaching its forty-one thatched roofs and cutting deep shadows into its maze of lanes and paths. It followed Ba Pe as he left the north gate of the village to stroll down the main path to the south gate, the rifle slung over his shoulder, but it failed to reveal the man hiding behind the pagoda outside the gates who had been told that an American lived in this village and might help him.

The moon shining on her face woke Gen Ferris, or perhaps it was the manic cries of a cuckoo in the trees beyond the compound. She stirred and her eyes flicked open to move drowsily around a room blurred by the shroud of mosquito netting under which she lay. She found the faces of the American movie stars on the left wall: Doris Day and Joanne Dru, Dan Dailey and Bing Crosby, and on the right wall the watchful eyes of the marionette that Htun Schwae had carved and costumed for her in miniature: Zawgwi the alchemist, the all-powerful lord of magic and sorcery, his red clothes and his red wand the color of blood in the moonlight. *But Htun Schwae,* she had protested, *doesn't your carving Zawgwi small in size make his power small?* and Htun Schwae had looked at her gravely and said, *Does your being small in size make your power small, Zen?*

Now she remembered that tomorrow was special because it was said that a river steamer from Rangoon was on its way and would be reaching Theingyu around noon, the first steamer in months; it was rumored that Europeans were aboard and it had been a long time since she had seen a European. She smiled, not aware of San Ya's horoscopes or of such matters as omens. Her eyes closed and she slept, the smile lingering on her small-boned white face made paler by moonlight.

The next day the rumors of a steamer proved to be true but whether it was also true that it carried Europeans could not be substantiated because the steamer did not stop at Theingyu, which was seen as ominous because this had never happened before. Gen stood and waited on the shore with Mi-Mi, who

3

had brought food to sell the passengers; the long plank that substituted for a gangway was ready to be lifted into place when the shabby old blue and white riverboat steamed around the curve in the Irrawaddy, leaving a triumphant wake behind it. Murmurs of pleasure rose from the villagers lining the river's bank: smiles, laughs of delight blossomed, and a sense of excitement. But the steamer's speed had not diminished and it was Mr. San Ya who first expressed dismay. Slowly the murmurs of delight faded, and with it Gen's hope of seeing a European. However, because of the boat the Japanese had sunk in the middle of the river during the war, the steamer had to sail tantalizingly close to the shore and it was possible to search out the faces of the people lining the rails. Straining to see, Gen thought she found a woman who might be European, sitting very erect in a deck chair, dressed all in silky gray with hair to match, but it was no more than a glimpse for people kept getting in her way. What drew her gaze at last was a Burmese standing at the rail who seemed to be staring directly at Gen. Her gaze returned to him and she became very still, puzzled by the way he regarded her, as if she was familiar to him. He was a small plump man with a brown face. It was disconcerting—she felt hypnotized by those eyes—and then he released her by turning his head away and she wondered at its happening at all, even as something deep inside her whispered, *I will see that man again . . .* and then the steamer turned midstream, the faces became profiles and then disappeared as the boat proceeded on to Kyaikkasan, five miles upstream.

Mi-Mi turned to her with eyes anxious for her friend. "No Ingalei, no Ameiyikan, Zen."

Gen said, *"Keissa masibu*—never mind," and hid her face by leaning over and picking up little Ah Par, who squealed with delight.

4

But to Mr. San Ya the steamer not stopping was seen as another omen, and in the afternoon, while the men worked in the fields and while Mr. San Ya—being a man of *pon*—played dominoes with Htun Schwae in the shade of a neem tree, the foreigner in their village, Gen's father, ended his life with a bullet in his head, which proved in the most unfortunate manner that he had owned a gun after all.

2

HER TRUE NAME was Genevieve Beauchamp Ferris but ow-
ing to a difference in phonetics among the Burmese she was
known to them as Zen, and her last name pronounced as Perris,
and Zen Perris she had become to everyone except her father.
She was sixteen years old but looked twelve, except when her
small face turned pinched, at which time Ma Nu, who cooked
for them, said she looked like a little old woman. In the five
years they had lived in Theingyu her father had rarely been
seen; it was known from Ma Nu that he tutored Zen when he
was well, suffered recurring bouts of malaria and was engaged
in writing a book, although about this Ma Nu was skeptical
because she never saw him at work. In the meantime Zen was
nurtured by Ma Nu and by the villagers, and trudged up and
down the lanes in her odd felt hat and ragged sneakers, grave
and self-contained as she visited Htun Schwae to see his mario-

nettes, or helped Mi-Mi sweep the courtyard of the nearby monastery to gain merit.

The gray felt hat was all that she had of her mother, who had died of typhoid during the Japanese occupation, and the sneakers were the gift of an aunt in America whom she had never seen but who sent wonderful magazines that Zen shared with the village, so that in nearly every house, in company with a picture of Aung San who had been assassinated at the time of Independence, there hung small pictures of movie stars and of American advertisements for Coca-Cola ("Refreshment Is Sincerely Yours With Ice-Cold Coca Cola for 5¢") and Tangee lipstick ("for lips men love and love to kiss") and Noxzema Beauty Cream ("are blemishes giving YOU an inferiority complex?")

Now it was left to Ma Nu to tell Zen what had happened during this long dusty hot afternoon. She found her down by the river mending a net with Maung Au, who caught fish for the village and was therefore a low Buddhist because he took life. When Ma Nu told her that her father was dead Zen gave a queer little cry and flung out a hand in protest, as if to ward off such news, and then her face tightened, she straightened her shoulders and walked silently back to the house with Ma Nu.

They buried Gen's father three hours after his death, quickly and in a grave outside the village because it was believed that such a violent premature death would bring harm to the village, that the spirit of Mr. Ferris, unripe for departure, might remain behind to haunt their dreams, bring a poor rice harvest or disease to the villagers. There were no *pongyi* summoned from the monastery, in spite of Gen's filling their rice bowls each morning; in such cases there was not even a coffin but out of deference to Zen a rough coffin was constructed by two of the young

men and they carried her father to the shallow grave on the hill
with only Zen in attendance. Not even Ma Nu dared go with
her but waited by the village gate, fingering her prayer necklace
with its one hundred and eight beads.

The sun was setting in an eruption of fire and gilt and saffron
and pink, and the rooks were circling the thorn trees, twittering
and scolding but not quite blurring the sound of the temple bell
from the monastery beyond the next hill; it was the time of day
that Gen had always loved most, but as Maung Au and Aung
Thoo lowered the coffin into the ground and tossed stones and
earth over it her face was stern. Finished, they waited for her
but she shook her head.

"*Ceizu timbade*—thank you," she said, and they left to immediately wash their hands of the dirt from this unripe green
death. When they had gone Gen frowned. There were no tears
in her: she had been thrown on her own resources for so long,
for half of her sixteen-year-old life, that a whole cast of charac-
ters named Genevieve had never been allowed entry—small
genevieves that in the course of growing up normally would
have surfaced and might even have flowered; they had been
replaced by a Genevieve who was self-reliant, practical, cheerful, and who sometimes felt a stranger even to herself.

She was being practical now, thinking not of her father but of
the steamer that had passed Theingyu today, and of how it
would be tied up for the night at a village not too far away, and
of how in a few days it would begin its trip back to Rangoon.
Her father had not been so uncaring as might first have been
assumed: she had understood this when she unwrapped the
small pile he left for her on the table and had found the bank
book: almost all of their money was gone. Soon after they had
come to Theingyu he'd shown her the account book with its
four figures and he had explained that here was the money for

their return to the United States and for Gen's first years at college. Now the figures had shrunk to three and there was barely enough for one passage out of the country to America.

Other than the account book, her father had bequeathed her the address of her aunt in New York City, Gen's birth certificate, a passport issued in New York in 1934 with a photo of her mother and father holding a two-month-old child who was Gen, his gold pocket watch, eight hundred *kyat* and a note that read: *It's time for me to go, Gen. If you can get to Rangoon there'll be help. Go to New York—I couldn't—and God bless you.*

He had not signed it; they had never known each other very well and he was not a man to show affection but he had told her to go to Rangoon, and it was of Rangoon that she was thinking. Eight hundred kyat wouldn't last long, it was less than a hundred dollars in U.S. money but she thought it would buy passage on the steamer to Rangoon, and food for the long trip downstream, and once in Rangoon she had the bank book to prove enough money for passage to America. There was the old bicycle in the shed behind the house and if she left early in the morning, at sunrise, she could peddle north and look for the steamer.

It was the efficient thing to do, before the money ran out.

"Lai labala?" called Ma Nu.

"Cecchin," she called back.

The sun had slipped behind the trees, leaving the sky a luminous mother-of-pearl with tender strokes of fading mauve and saffron. With a last look at the grave she turned and walked down the hill to Ma Nu, who saw that her face was pinched again, like that of an old woman.

"You will live with me, you can be my *thami* now," Ma Nu told her.

"Ma Nu, you already have two daughters and three sons,"

9

she pointed out. And no land, she might have added, so that Ma Nu's husband had to work for Mr. San Ya in his paddies.

"Then you can still live in your house, there is money for rice?"

Gen shook her head. "There's a little money but—*masaluppabu*—it isn't enough to live on," she said. "I will have to leave, Ma Nu, my father has written, 'go to Yangoun.'"

"*Bedo?*"

"Soon," she said.

"*Khimbya tay autthe mathwabane!*" protested Ma Nu.

She didn't tell her that of course she must go alone, nor did she mention her determination to leave in the morning; still another goodbye was more than she could bear. Ma Nu walked with her through the lane to the compound and stopped, quietly pointed to the lamp she'd left burning, reminded her to eat well of the fish and rice prepared for her, and with a last anxious glance at Gen continued on to her house to feed her own family.

Leaving the gate open Gen walked into the compound which was occupied by sheds and a few straggly plants. Unlike the other houses in the village—built high off the ground with only three walls—the house in which she and her father lived had four walls for privacy and three rooms: a large main room with a small bedroom on either side of it; the kitchen, in the usual village fashion, was outside so that cooking odors would never invade the house. In the main room Ma Nu had left the kerosene lamp burning, its light very small against the dark walls. Gen lit a candle from it and carried it into her own room to begin heaping her few belongings on the bed.

She had taken Zawgwi down from his peg and was carefully tying his marionette strings when a shadow suddenly leaped up the wall in front of her and hung there. She'd heard no steps

and no one had called out to her . . . she spun around to see a
man standing in the doorway watching her, a stranger and what
was most astonishing of all a European. He was an alarming
sight, unshaven, a bloody gash across one cheek, his rough cot-
ton trousers torn across the knee. He said, "I was told there's an
American in this village." His voice was hoarse, his face tanned
to the color of his dark hair and he was wearing Burmese
clothes except for a glorious pair of laced-up leather boots on
which her eyes lingered for a moment before returning to his
face. She said gravely, "You look awful, you'd better sit down,
hadn't you?"

"So you *are* American." He limped to the bed and sat on the
edge of it. "I saw you up on the hill where someone was getting
buried and you *looked* American . . . I followed you back. I
don't suppose there's any food handy, I haven't eaten in days."
He thought about this. "No, there was a banana yesterday, it
fell off someone's ox cart. God it tasted good."

"Yes," she said, knowing that kind of hunger. "Wait here a
minute."

She returned with the dinner Ma Nu had left for her. "I shall
have to eat some of it," she told him frankly, "because I'm
leaving in the morning and I won't be able to bicycle very far if
I don't eat tonight."

"Leaving?" he said blankly. "What do you mean leaving?"

She said in a matter-of-fact voice, "It was my father who was
buried on the hill tonight."

The hand he was plunging into the rice bowl stopped in mid-
air. "Oboy," he said and looked at her, really seeing her for the
first time. What he thought he saw was a thin child with a face
shadowed by a gray felt hat and wearing a blouse and short skirt
of indeterminate color; light from the candle fell on thin wrists
and hands and while it shadowed her legs he could clearly see

the sneakers from which the canvas had been cut to allow room for her toes. Having announced that her father was dead her chin had gone up an inch and she had straightened her shoulders, but neither made her taller or fatter. "That's hard luck," he said, and then thinking of his own situation, "You're all that's left?"

She nodded.

"Where are you going, for pete's sake, and you said *bicycling?*"

In a cool precise voice she told him about the steamer. "It didn't stop here today, which it should have done, which means it may not stop here on the way back to Rangoon, so I'm going to go and look for it. If I can get to Rangoon—"

He interrupted. "You mean there's a boat, a steamer, and it sails down the Irrawaddy straight to Rangoon? Is it safe?"

She nodded. "I think so. There are always government soldiers aboard with machine guns, I counted at least ten today when it passed. It's the first boat since the rainy season so they must have thought in Rangoon it was safe."

He whistled. "It sounds good." He swallowed a piece of fish and held out the bowl to her. "Here—you eat some."

She took the bowl, absently forming rice into a ball and neatly, efficiently dispatching it down her throat.

He said thoughtfully, "We could go together . . ."

She lifted her face and gave him a look that surprised him: he was not accustomed to being appraised so coolly, and from a child it was unexpected. "How did you get hurt?" she asked.

"A bullet," he said impatiently. "Yunnan's sent out a description of me, so now the White Flag Communists are after me and for all I know the Red Flags too. I was supposed to escape into Thailand but I trusted the wrong people and ended up in the wrong country."

"What were you doing in China?" she asked, calmly finishing the fish.

"Why should I tell you? Look here, do you have to wear that fool hat?"

"Yes."

"Stubborn child. All right, I was gathering information, is that enough for you? I assume you're aware that Chiang Kai-shek fled China for Taiwan last year and the Communists have won their revolution. At the moment they seem to be doing their best to take over your country, too—I mean this country."

"You mean you're a spy."

He shrugged. "If you want to call it that. Look, you can help me, you know the language, don't you? I can help you, too—you shouldn't be heading north alone, it's dangerous, insurgents everywhere."

"There's only one bicycle," she said, considering this, "but I suppose if we walked we could follow the river better." Her voice brightened. "And we could leave tonight if there are two of us, instead of waiting for daylight." With a last shred of fish she efficiently wiped the dish clean. "I don't mind if you come too, but you can't go like that. My father's shaving cream and razor are in his room," she told him. "You could wash the blood off your face while I finish packing."

"Good girl," he said, but he didn't move. "You're pretty cool for a girl who's just lost her father, aren't you? What did he die of?"

Without expression she said, "He shot himself."

Appalled, he stared at her. "Why would he do that, and leave you here alone?"

"I think there was no longer any money for us both to go back to America," she said.

"He sacrificed himself for you, then?"

13

She said seriously, "He was really quite a selfish person—I think most unhappy people are, don't you?—so it's hard to know." She added calmly, "I think it was his *kan* to go, because his spirit had become so unhappy."

"Hey," he said, shocked, "you're speaking of a dead man and your father."

"Yes of course," she said, giving him a puzzled look.

Primitive little beast, he thought. "How would you know his spirit was unhappy?"

She said gravely, "I think because he'd stopped believing in God."

"That sounds damned pious."

"Well, you see he was a missionary," she added politely.

And that, he thought, was *that.*

"Just the same, I wish—" A sigh escaped her and she leaned forward, thin arms clasping her knees.

"Wish what?" he asked, wondering what next.

"When Mr. San Ya's brother died in Mandalay," she said wistfully, "oh he was very rich, a man of pon, a *lugyi*—a big man, that is—his body was burned into ashes, just like the kings here, like royalty, I forget the word for it." She was silent, thinking about this, and a tiny smile curved her lips. "If my father hadn't killed himself—yes, if he'd died of malaria as Ma Nu thought last year—" Her chin went up. "I would have spent all the kyat he left on such a funeral, and given a great feast for the village."

He sat down again on the edge of the bed. "So you did love him."

He had startled her but out of respect for this stranger she considered the word. In Rangoon after her mother had died, one of the missionaries had questioned her at length about her feelings but she had thought them none of his business, and while not exactly telling him so she had made this clear. She was not accustomed to talking about feelings but she found at last an honest word to say. "There was a thread between us."

He nodded. "A bond, then, okay. Yes I understand." What the hell, he thought, and out of a generosity he'd not felt for a long time he said, "So why don't we give your father a royal funeral before we go? We could, you know."

He noticed that her hands were trembling—not so calm after all, he told himself—and now they moved convulsively. "Could we, could we really?"

"Why not? I've been lying out by that pagoda for two days, I wouldn't mind some digging if you've a shovel. There aren't any trees up on that hill, we'd have to carry the coffin down here but that shed in the back looks highly flammable. And we couldn't linger," he added sternly. "I mustn't be seen here; if insurgents capture this village your friends could be accused of hiding me."

She nodded. "There's a shovel in the back, I'll go and get it. A lantern, too?"

As she paused in the doorway for his answer the light from the candle entered the shadows under her hat and he saw her face: the thin delicate features, the eyes glittering with reflected candleshine. He said, "How old are you, anyway?"

"Sixteen."

"Cripes, *not* a child. But so thin!"

She nodded. "Ma Nu says it was the war."

He said caustically, "In the two days I've hidden behind that pagoda I haven't seen any natives that thin."

She said matter-of-factly, "We weren't here in Theingyu for the war." A startled look crossed her face. "What should I call you, what's your name?"

"I'm Neil Hamlin, I'm twenty-six and what's your name?"

"They call me Zen here, Zen Perris," she said, and left to bring back the shovel. When she returned he was bent nearly double over the mirror in her father's room, his face carved in yellow by the candle he'd placed under the mirror to shave his jaw. She had brought back not only the shovel but food as well, which she proceeded to wrap and stow away in her father's old knapsack: a pound of rice, peanuts, a precious tin of condensed milk, a handful of chick peas, and tea leaves wrapped in oiled paper. "There's a sweater of my father's that might fit you," she told him.

"Sweater? Thank God! Where?"

"In the corner hanging from a peg."

With this she returned to her own room to pack her treasures in a woven shoulder bag: the last magazine she'd received from her aunt, dated October 1949; a book of child's crossword puzzles, a pencil, a knife, matches, the papers her father had bequeathed her, the slingshot she always carried with her, and last of all the beloved figure of Zawgwi.

When he joined her she regarded him measuringly for a moment, studying the American look of him and comparing him with the photographs of movie stars on her wall, but it was quite hopeless, he merely looked solid, square-jawed and plain. He did, however, look honest and responsible. "I'm ready," she said, he nodded and they left the house.

This time the front gate entering the maze of village lanes was to be avoided; Gen led him through the gate at the back of the compound and out into the fields. The huge arc of darkening sky still held brush strokes of color from the sun's passage; there was a sense of drama, of suspense in this change from day to night, the birds silent, the moon round and pale in the east, waiting to emerge onstage with the pale stars. A dog barked. An owl hooted, a faint breeze stirred the trees. Gen pointed to the grave and he began digging into the earth until the coffin was exposed.

"Now the hard part," he said, fervently hoping the coffin would hold together. Carefully, gently, he pried the box from its hollow, and down the hill they struggled with it, not daring to show a light, stopping often to rest. Through the rear gate they carried the coffin and now Gen took over, for having built the shed herself she knew how to quickly disassemble its reed and thatch. When a pyre had been built the coffin was lifted to the top.

Hamlin said, "Before we light the fire bring everything here for a quick retreat and place it by the gate."

She nodded and carried knapsack and shoulder bag to the rear of the compound. When she returned he handed her a match; the moment had arrived. "This is your baby," he said cryptically.

She held the match, looking gravely at the pile of bamboo and straw. "I don't know what to say, but something—*something* should be said . . ." And lifting her voice she recited, " 'To everything there is a season—and a time to every purpose under the heaven: a time to be born and a time to die.' " Her voice faltered and then to his surprise she closed her eyes and said, " 'I take refuge in the Buddha, I take refuge in the Dharma, I take refuge in the Sangha . . .' "

She opened her eyes, struck the match and lit the straw.

"Okay—*let's go!*" he shouted.

They ran with the sound of flames crackling greedily behind them, ran out of the compound through the fields and across the road, passed the shadowed pagoda with its *stupa* gleaming under the rising moon, and stopped only when they reached the edge of the forest. There, panting, they looked back at flames pouring into the sky, silhouetting walls, trees and roofs, and then as they watched the brilliance flared, weakened and sank down behind the walls, leaving only a dull glow.

And suddenly all the feeling that Gen had dispatched to distant regions of the heart rose in her in outraged protest and she burst into tears. Great and terrible sobs assaulted her as she wept at last, violently, while Neil Hamlin held her, awkwardly patting her shoulder from moment to moment, and hoping like hell he'd not made a mistake in joining forces with this weeping child.

3

THE STEAMER *Khayioe* ran aground twelve miles above the village of Kyaikkasan. The river had not been completely cleared of debris in the five years since the war had ended and further attempts had been abandoned after Independence, when insurgency erupted and steamer service had to be suspended for weeks at a time. Now with the rainy season ended the wing of a downed Zero fighter plane had slowly edged its way loose, twisted and drifted up from the riverbed, dusk rendering it nearly invisible. Once it was seen the tiller was thrust hard to starboard, the steamer missed the obstacle by inches, but in turning shoreward it met the muddy shallows of the riverbank with a thud and reverberating tremors.

For Lady Waring this was nearly the last straw: she had been seven days aboard the *Khayioe,* they had been shot at by insurgents, stunned by heat during the day, chilled by night, and in

spite of there being two others in her party to harass, she was
bored. She had waited weeks in Rangoon for transport to Mandalay, but Mandalay was currently in the hands of the Karens,
the rail line had been cut and plane service canceled; she had
begun to envision spending the entire dry season in Rangoon.
Hearing rumors that a steamer might be leaving soon with arms
for the government soldiers she had made daily rounds of the
Ministry of Information, the Special Branch of police, the British Consulate and the shipping lines, alternately cajoling, threatening and bribing, making it quite clear that she had connections in London and at Buckingham Palace, and that she was
accustomed to having her own way.

In the end a permit for travel into Upper Burma on the
Khayioe had been issued but the British Consul, aware of the
precariousness of his position—and of those connections in London—had insisted on young Culpepper accompanying Lady
Waring and her secretary on an official basis. The Ministry, the
police and the shipping company having submitted, they ac-
knowledged defeat and issued permits to the handful of other
Europeans besieging them; it was hoped that by the time the
steamer reached Mandalay the government forces would be in
control again but if not it was thought that unleashing Lady
Waring upon the insurgents would not be without benefit.

When the last shudder of boat meeting shore had died away,
Lady Waring lifted her cane and pointed it at Mr. Culpepper.
"You," she said. "Kindly approach the captain and see what he
plans to do now and how long this will delay us."

Culpepper said cheerfully, "I suspect he's rather busy just
now." He had learned in seven days that the only possible insu-
lation against Lady Waring was to (1) pretend to misunderstand
her, (2) pretend not to hear her, or (3) surround himself with a

deadening and quite unrealistic cheerfulness, which he was displaying now.

"Then try eavesdropping," said Lady Waring tartly. "You said you'd learned a little Burmese—practice it."

The steamer's accident had been accepted calmly enough by the natives aboard the *Khayioe*. Having rushed to the rail they retired now to the corners they'd staked out on the deck with their rugs, blankets, flowers and baskets of food. Lady Waring had observed them for seven days, marveling at their stamina, their obvious enjoyment of this endless trip, the babies fed and played with, the dice and dominoes engrossing husbands and soldiers, some of them vanishing into the villages at which they stopped every night to be replaced by new faces, new babies, new husbands and children. When the steamer had been machine-gunned from the shore they had preserved their calm, simply moving to the opposite side of the deck or taking refuge behind crates or boxes while the soldiers lazily returned fire from the boat. There seemed to be a distressing lack of worry among them, which she supposed was due to their equally distressing beliefs in the Buddha. Nothing seemed to worry them, not even sleeping on the deck, which was surprisingly open to attack, the so-called Europeans—actually most of them were Americans—occupying the three cabins squeezed into the stern, a cabin Lady Waring had to share with the silent, pretty Miss Thorald, who was at least civil enough to be quiet, and with Mrs. Caswell, who dithered and faltered and seemed apologetic for her very existence.

Culpepper returned, smiling his obnoxiously cheerful smile. "We're being asked to go ashore to lighten the weight of the boat," he said, "and the soldiers are going to heave and push. If that fails, someone will walk to the next village and bring back

21

ropes, and probably bullocks, and more men to do the heaving and pushing."

She surprised him by only shrugging. "A welcome change. Ask my secretary—Moreland—to carry my deck chair ashore, if you will."

Once ensconced in her chair, Lady Waring observed the scene around her with her usual jaundiced eye. The Caswell couple were wandering up and down the shore, pointing into the trees and examining the clusters of tiny orchids. Pompous ass, thought Lady Waring, and shifted her gaze to his wife, who looked drowned, as so many women did who married overbearing and dominating husbands. The silent Miss Thorald had seated herself on the fallen trunk of a tree and was reading a book. Culpepper and her secretary Moreland were discussing birds: words like *pied-crested cuckoo, iora* and *Bengal brown fish-owl* reached her, but Lady Waring realized that the natives and the countryside had begun to interest her more than her compatriots. For the children this was playtime, and without the slightest embarrassment they were naked in the shallows, their wet flesh gleaming like mahogany; the men, still wearing their *longyis,* were pouring water over themselves, several women crouched in the water washing clothes while older boys watched with glee the efforts to back the steamer off the sandbank.

Her gaze went beyond them to the river that ran like pale silk in the late afternoon light. On the distant shore a water buffalo stood patiently in the shallows while a man stood in an ox cart and filled barrels with water. Beyond him lay the tender green fields stretching to blue hills, on one of which the sun caught and picked out the tip of a pagoda. She supposed the scene had looked no different a hundred years ago.

She had been prepared to find her journey nearly intolerable and the country primitive and boring. Fed on the hostility of the colonial attitude toward all darker-skinned subjects of the British Empire, she found it difficult to admit now that she was stirred by the tranquillity and the sense of timelessness that she was meeting here. She was tired—from grief, from the war, from change, but a knowledge had begun growing in her that she was being overtaken by something that reached out to her tired spirit and caressed it, stroked it, gave a more enduring light to her memories and offered healing.

I'm not sure I want to be healed, she thought peevishly, and wondered if she had grown too accustomed to pain.

She rose from her chair. "I'm going to walk a little," she announced to her secretary.

Moreland only smiled and nodded but Miss Thorald, hearing her, looked up from her book. "I'd like that, may I join you?"

Mr. Baharian, strolling barefooted up from the shore, overheard her and said, "Give me a minute to put on my shoes and I'll go with you."

Outrageous man, thought Lady Waring with distaste; he had tied a length of silk around his head and looked like a pirate; what was worse, the prim and fastidious Mr. Gunfer, as narrow as Mr. Baharian was huge, at once announced that he would walk, too, and Mr. Caswell, hearing of their plans, paused beside Culpepper and Moreland and said to his wife, "There now, Helen, you can walk with Lady Waring, too, it'll do you good to stretch your legs."

"There's a small path over there," said Miss Thorald. "Perhaps it will lead to a village."

Mrs. Caswell said eagerly, "There's either a pagoda or a *nat* shrine that we glimpsed through the trees. Perhaps we could investigate!"

The small group set out up the narrow path between the

tamarinds and the palms, a plump brown-faced Burmese following them.

Dusk began to creep slowly over the river and darken bright silver into pewter, the boat gave one final shudder and broke free of the sandbank to the sound of cheering. The gangplank was set up again, the Burmese swarmed aboard, chattering and laughing, the steamer blew its horn and Mr. Caswell, Culpepper and Moreland hurried aboard, still talking. It was several minutes before it was noticed that Lady Waring's deck chair remained standing on the empty shore, and it was nearly dark before it was discovered that five of the Europeans were missing.

4

"I'M SORRY," Gen said, drawing away from Hamlin's awkward comforting arm and wiping her tears with a sleeve.

"Look, when was the last time you cried?" he demanded.

She gave him a wan smile and hiccuped. It was a fair question and for a second she wrestled with her terror at having lost control, pitted against a feeling of lightness and delicious exhaustion. She said solemnly, "It's like vomit, isn't it."

He shook his head. "You sure have a weird way of expressing things but I suppose the analogy applies: both have to come out. Or up." He picked up the knapsack and slung it over his shoulder. "Let's go, okay?"

She nodded and turned for a last glance at Theingyu, asleep again in the moonlight. "Yes, but up ahead we should cross the road and walk near the river," she told him. "We can walk faster across the fields."

The night was dark but it was the soft velvety darkness of Burma: the moon having reached its zenith the night before it had entered the time of *la byigyaw,* the waning moon, but the stars were no less brilliant, scattered across the sky like handfuls of glittering sequins. They walked in silence, two very small figures moving in and out of shadows under the vast panorama of night sky, Hamlin carrying the knapsack and Gen her Shan shoulder bag. The moon that had hung over the low hills in the west moved slowly into the sky and cut a gleaming swath of silver across the Irrawaddy. They bypassed several villages, inspiring a number of dogs to bark, and stopped at last to rest inside a dense grove of bamboo, welcomed by the mournful cry of an owl.

Without speaking Hamlin rummaged in the knapsack and drew out his precious flask of water and a pot. Borrowing her knife he began digging a hole in the earth, scooping out soil with his hands. Breaking silence Gen said, "What's that for?"

"A fire. Old American Indian trick, build the fire in the ground so no flames can be seen. See if you can find some dry twigs."

As the fire ignited she held out her hands to its warmth and Hamlin again saw how they trembled, as if she repressed much more than grief. She watched Hamlin pour water in the pot and place it over the hole; opening the knapsack she dropped in a handful of rice, the muted glow from the flames barely illuminating their faces as they warmed themselves, waiting, silent.

It was several minutes before they realized they were not alone.

There were three of them standing in the shadows, three men wearing torn remnants of uniform, each holding a rifle pointed at them. Gen said, "Oh!" in a small voice and jumped to her feet.

26

Hamlin rose more slowly, saying, "Who are you? What do you want?"

"*Hei—Ingalei,*" said the eldest, and explained this to his companions, regarding Gen and Hamlin benevolently but edging closer and closer as he spoke until he reached the knapsack and knelt beside it. Opening it he exclaimed, "*Cizan!—shan!*"

Hamlin looked to Gen for translation but she refused his glance, remaining stubbornly silent, her face shuttered. Only when they picked up her shoulder bag and brought out the puppet Zawgwi did she cry out, "No—oh, no!"

They gave her a startled glance and then returned to spilling out the bags' contents. At sight of the roll of kyat they turned gleeful, counting it. When everything lay spread out on the ground—the sack of rice, the tea and milk, peanuts, Zawgwi, Gen's papers, passport and money—the eldest began issuing orders. Food, papers, money and puppet were stuffed back into the two bags and handed to the youngest with fresh orders. He nodded and vanished soundlessly into the darkness.

"*Pyanjazou,*" the leader said, and with a mocking salute to Gen and Hamlin, he and his companion disappeared into the woods, too.

"Damn," exploded Hamlin when they'd gone. "If only we'd had a gun! Damn it, they've taken everything!"

"Yes," she said in a tight voice.

"I didn't enjoy feeling so helpless. Damn it, if only we'd had a *gun.*"

She nodded. "We have to get it back."

"Back how?" he said angrily. "They've gone!"

"They have my steamer money," she said, "and they have the passport and the bank book and they have Zawgwi." She looked dazed. "They've taken everything."

"I've already said that," he told her irritably. "Why the hell didn't you speak to them in their language? You could at least have explained that your papers are of no value to them!"

"They would still have taken my money for the boat, I have to get it back," she repeated.

"Great," he said sarcastically. "How?"

She said slowly, "It is good the dacoits didn't know I understood them because they talked freely. They've been out all night, they have no food and they're hungry. They sent the young one, the boy, back to the pagoda—his name is Chi Ti—to cook rice for them while they meet a friend two miles away and return with him."

"So they're hungry, fine, I'm hungry too, but—" He stopped. "You said *pagoda?*"

In the light of the dying fire her eyes gleamed like cat's eyes. She nodded. "I am no longer stunned, U Hamlin, we will get back the rice and my money—we must!"

He nodded. "I'm hungry enough to try anything for that rice but what pagoda? There seem to be pagodas everywhere."

"I know a little of the road here because I went sometimes to Mandalay with U San Ya before it was captured by the Karens," she said. "At the bend of the road ahead there is a pagoda on a hilltop, and there is also the pagoda we passed half a mile ago. Do you know Christian prayers, U Hamlin?"

"Why?"

"You should pray they will be hiding in one of those two."

He said grimly, "We've not much time to find the right pagoda before the others get back." He tossed earth over the fire. "Let's go."

"No—wait! Have you a coin, U Hamlin?"

He groped in the pocket of his trousers and brought up a Chinese fen. "What for?"

28

"If the thamma deva that Ma Nu says watches over me will speak, it will tell us at which pagoda they've camped."

"Thamma deva!"

"Oh yes." Grasping the coin she closed her eyes, her lips moving without sound; opening them she said, "If the side of the coin with the 2 on it comes up we will go to the pagoda ahead of us, if not to the pagoda already passed." She tossed it in the air, caught it and showed it to him. "We will find them camped at the pagoda on the hilltop up ahead."

"You believe this stuff?" he said incredulously. "What's a thamma deva?"

"A spirit who helps."

He gave her a wary glance. "Well, I suppose without a gun we can use any help we can get."

They hurried out of the wood into the moonlight again, crossed the road and began making their way toward the wooded hill in the distance on which the silhouette of a pagoda could be seen. Ascending the hill through the woods they moved silently, not stopping until they reached its crest and came out on cleared ground near the pagoda.

Hamlin grabbed her arm. "Look!" he whispered. "You were right."

It was an ancient pagoda, neglected and crumbling, shaped like a bell with two broad terraces surrounding it. Under one of the terraces a hole had been cut, making an entrance to the small relic chamber inside. From this cavelike hole a faint glow could be seen; someone had built a fire in the crevice under the pagoda.

"Let me find a stick," whispered Hamlin. "I need a weapon."

"But he has a rifle," she whispered back, "and he will hear us. Let me see if I can make him come out."

"He won't come out," Hamlin said flatly. "Why should he?"

"Wait," she said, and from deep in her throat there began a curious sound that moved higher and higher in pitch and volume. *"Ooooooooooooooo,"* she wailed. *"Ooooooooo . . . Chi Ti, Chi Ti . . ."* Her voice rose like a dirge, sank, turned into a piercing moan that sent chills down Hamlin's spine. He looked at her with respect and then at the cavelike opening where a head had appeared, etched black against the fire's red glow.

Chi Ti called nervously, *"Badu—Maung Anu?"*

From Gen's throat there now came words, sad and mournful. *"Meisha-meisha! Kuthokan makaumbri . . . Chi Ti, Chi Ti— oooooooo."*

"Hto hamin aohla! Htohaminaloa!" cried Chi Ti and stumbled from the cave with his rifle, looking frantically around him.

Gen's voice sank and rose again, haunting, insistent, merciless.

Hamlin nudged her: in the moonlight a gauzy, misty shape was moving across the ground, swirling in strange eddies as if sucked by a wind—but there was no wind—and slowly gathering speed until as it approached the cave it gathered itself into a towering shape, a wraith, a huge shadow of a being with lifted arms and hunched shoulders. Hamlin, watching, put his hands to his eyes and rubbed them but when he looked again the shape was still there, swirling closer and closer to the boy at the cave.

Chi Ti, gaping at it, gave a terrified scream and fled.

"Good," said Gen matter-of-factly as he vanished into the woods. "Let's get my money."

Hamlin stood paralyzed. The mist had thinned and was floating gently a few feet above the earth now, slowly dispersing. "Ground mist," he muttered. *"Not a ghost, not a shape—but I saw a shape,"* he told himself. "I did, didn't I?"

He was still rooted there when Gen raced out of the cave

with knapsack and shoulder bag. "I have all but the rice he was cooking on the fire," she cried. "Come, we must run now." With a look at the sky, "It's nearing dawn, U Hamlin, we need a hiding place where we can see but not be seen. See the river. Watch for the steamer." She tugged at his arm. "Hurry, we must go!"

"Yes—yes of course," he said, feeling like a fool, and ran with her down the hill, leaving the pagoda behind.

In the light that precedes dawn they found what they needed: a small hill surrounded by fields on which stood a copse of trees to hide in, with the road not far below.

"Oh that was fun," she said as she sank down on the ground, and opening the knapsack she began sorting out the peanuts. "This is a *good* place to rest, we can even see a slice of river beyond those rice paddies."

He chose to seat himself with his back against a tree. Looking at her he said cautiously, "About that thamma deva."

She looked at him attentively. "Yes."

"Did you happen to notice anything unusual back at the cave while you were making noises like—like whatever?"

"Like a ghost. There *are* ghosts, you know, as well as nats and demons and devas in this country."

Amused, he said, "Only in this country, only in Burma?"

"I can't tell about other countries," she said politely, "I've only lived in this one."

Neatly blocked by this remark he backtracked. "Did your father know about this thamma deva that somebody says looks after you?"

"My father?" She looked surprised. "No, of course not, he was here to tell the Burmese what he believed and what he thought *they* should believe."

31

That frankness again; he chuckled. "I see . . . so he missed knowing about thamma devas. But you've not answered my question: did you notice anything unusual back at the cave?"

"Such as what?" she asked earnestly.

"The cloud of mist, for instance?"

"Ground mist," she said, nodding. "Yes there's often mist when the cold air meets the warm earth."

"You didn't see it—well, take on any shape?"

"Shape? The mist? My eyes were closed to concentrate on scaring Chi Ti out of the cave."

"And a remarkable job you did," he told her.

"What did you see?" she asked courteously.

"Never mind." He continued to eye her uneasily. "Look, can't you take that blasted hat off for a few minutes? Are you going to sleep in it? I can't see your eyes."

She removed the hat and he saw that she had straight brown hair cut raggedly with scissors just below the ears. He saw too that her eyes were gray-green. Plain as a broomstick, he thought, except for the eyes, which were bright and curious with a feather-stroke of eyebrow over each, yet even as he studied her face it changed, becoming older, tense and lived, and then he blinked and on second glance it was a child's face again, features delicately arranged on an oval that was waiting to be written on. A chameleon!

He said, "Now that I can see your eyes tell me again what a thamma deva is."

"Oh, devas are gods," she told him in her crisp little voice. "Once they were human beings who lived very good lives, such good lives they've been reborn as gods to help people. The king of them all—because there are many devas—is Thagyamin."

"Ever see one?" he asked casually.

She decided that she didn't care to talk about this, she knew very well what he had seen at the cave but a person didn't speak of these matters without offending the devas or courting the ill will of the nats. In an offhand voice she said, "My father used to say how different time is here, it used to make him angry, it moves so slowly here, you see. But I think when time moves slowly—" She hesitated. "I think when time moves very slowly it leaves spaces in between the moments for more things to happen. I've finished eating, I think I'll sleep for a few minutes," and having said this she abruptly lay down with her head on the knapsack and closed her eyes.

Hamlin remained upright, having done a fair amount of sleeping during his two days of hiding by the pagoda, and in any case he felt that one of them had to guard against dacoits creeping up to surprise them again. From where he sat with his back against the tree he could see the mist-shrouded river half a mile away, separated from him by the dusty road and by neat squares of paddies along the riverbank. Beyond the river the earth stretched flat to the hills where the tip of a hot orange sun was rising, brightening the sky but not the land as yet, so that the valley mist shrouding the base of the hills turned them into islands floating in the sky. He watched the sun clear the ridge of hills, trailing fronds of pink behind it and suffusing the sky with gold, watched it send out exploratory fingers of light until it reached the river and swept away the mist to reflect every blazing sunrise color in its calm surface.

To hell with devas and nats, he thought, this was dazzling. Off to his right his eye caught movement and he saw an ox cart take shape on the road below, raising clouds of dust. It turned into one of the checkered fields along the river, the farmer dismounted and presently—very small—he could be seen walking up and down the rows of stubble. The farmer was the only human to be seen in this vast sweep of landscape.

And what a landscape, mused Hamlin, as sunlight reached the fields below to restore their delicate shades of green and rich brown. The air was clear and cool and without heat as yet, and the birds were chattering. For a moment he reflected on the long way he'd traveled: from Xiagan in China across the mountains into Burma, through the jungles of the Shan country to Lashio, always hiding and never safe. He had skirted Mandalay —that had been tricky, he'd been seen, called by name and shot at there—and now he was here, briefly at rest on this endless journey and in hope of a river steamer if this girl was right, this strange girl with her felt hat and her devas. Of course the boat had not been sighted yet but he guessed they'd walked fewer than ten miles during the night; the dacoit attack had occupied them for too long a time.

Gen stirred and opened her eyes, awakened by a dream: in her dream she'd been standing on the shore again with Mi-Mi as the steamer passed, searching for European faces, her attention caught by the gaze of the plump little brown-faced man at the rail. In the dream his face had slowly moved toward her until it filled her vision and she had felt that in another minute she might drown in those huge, searching brown eyes. It was this that had awakened her; brushing away the dream she sat up. "Any sign of the steamer?"

He shook his head.

She said, "I can't sleep anymore, would you be afraid of being seen if we walk in daylight?"

"Yes," he said, making a face, "but I think it has to be done, we need that boat!"

"U Hamlin," she said sternly, looking into his face, "there is a proverb Ma Nu speaks of, that you can see a man carrying a

spear on his shoulder and walking, but you cannot see the fate
the man carries on his shoulders. What is your fate, U Hamlin?"

Amused, he shrugged. "How can I know, does anyone? I
suppose if I make it back to the United States I'll try again for a
job teaching Chinese history."

"You are not always a spy, then?"

"That's a leftover from the war, when I was in China under
General Stillwell."

"How do you know they have a description of you, are you
that important?"

He shrugged. "I suspect it's mostly a matter of face—their
losing it, I mean. They found out about me in Xiagan, they
know I got away and I'm a 'foreign devil,' a 'round-eyes.'
They'd like very much to stash me away in one of their prisons
or better still shoot me." He added in a startled voice, "Of
course I do know things." He laughed. "My God, I've been on
the run for so long I forget. On the other hand they can't know
for sure what I know."

Gen grinned. "That's a mixed-up sentence. What is it you
know?"

"I've learned they plan to send an army into Korea in the
spring or summer, which—considering all the tangles of treaties
and pacts—could mean a real war." He sighed. "And at the
moment—I *must* be tired—I couldn't care less."

"You are tired?"

"Of course I'm tired," he said impatiently, "I've been walking for weeks."

"How many weeks?"

"Good God, you want me to count? I left Xiagan in late
autumn and now it's turned January. Have *you* ever walked for
days?"

"Oh I don't know," she said vaguely.

"What does that mean?"

Her eyes were on the farmer in the fields below. "We walked for quite a few days to get away from the Japanese: from Maymyo—that's a hill town north of Mandalay—down to Rangoon, where the Japanese caught us. Of course once in a while we were given a ride in an ox cart."

"Japanese," he repeated, staring at her. "My God, you were here during the war? I didn't stop to think you might have been here, I supposed you fled the country like most foreigners. What happened after the Japanese found you?"

"Oh, we were interned—in Rangoon for three years, in a compound."

"When was this?"

Under her hat he watched her eyebrows draw together in a frown. "I was eight so that would have been 1942."

"How were you treated?"

She said cautiously, "There wasn't much to eat and there was no medicine but they didn't beat anyone, and some were friendly. We were in a compound with other missionaries." She smiled suddenly. "My father called us a gaggle of missionaries but—" Her smile faded. "But that was when he was funny and cheerful, before my mother died."

Jarred by this casual statement Hamlin said, "She died in camp?"

"Yes, of typhoid."

Hamlin was appalled; he also realized that he was experiencing a rush of outrage at this man who had been her father. "Then can you tell me why the hell—after all that—your father didn't take the both of you back to the United States the minute the war ended?"

Gen explained it calmly. "He was in the hospital in Rangoon at first—with malaria, you see—and then he decided we should go back to the missionary station in Maymyo where we lived before the Japanese came, so we started out for Maymyo." She shrugged. "We got as far as Theingyu when he was sick with malaria again, and after that he stopped talking about Maymyo and said we'd go back to America as soon as he felt well enough."

He said skeptically, "And he never felt well enough?"

"I think he became frightened. Perhaps when one loses God this happens. Are you married, U Hamlin?" she asked, turning a solemn face toward him.

Startled he said, "Married! No, why?"

"I was thinking that perhaps you could marry me so I could go back to America with you."

He laughed in spite of himself. "Look, it doesn't work that way, Zen." Seeing her face he said gently, "Scared?"

Reaching into her shoulder bag she brought out her magazine and handed it to him. "Is it like this?"

"What on earth," he said. "A magazine for teenage girls?"

"Yes, there is an aunt I've never seen who sends these to me."

"Well I'm glad to hear you've an aunt somewhere, you'll be going to her, I assume?"

She nodded without interest and said seriously, "Have you attended a pajama party, U Hamlin?"

With equal seriousness he assured her that he had not, and lest this diminish her opinion of him he hastened to remind her that he'd not been in the United States for over a year but that he was sure he would have been invited to a pajama party if he'd been available. After riffling through a few pages with photographs of pretty girls in ruffles and curls he hazarded a quick glance at Gen in her tattered sneakers, battered hat and dusty clothes and understood her anxiety. This struck him as

37

rather hilarious because—having no sisters—he was accustomed
to looking on male-female relationships as adversarial, a matter
of coolly outmaneuvering these flirtatious creatures of artifice
and guile; now it struck him for the first time that Gen was
female, if still a child, and he was feeling for her not only sympathy but empathy. It was an educational moment for him. He
handed the magazine back to her and said dryly, "Don't worry,
just be yourself, which in itself will surprise people. What are
you scowling about?"

Gen's eyes were fixed upon the farmer walking in his fields
below them. She said, "I think I should go down and ask that
man if he's seen the steamer, and when. He looks safe to ask."

"Does it matter if he's seen the boat?"

She nodded. "I think so. We can't always walk close to the
river because you'd be seen by too many people in the villages.
If we should miss seeing the boat—"

"Then for pete's sake don't walk straight down the hill," he
told her. "Circle back and approach him from the road."

She placed her hat squarely on her head and rummaged in
her shoulder bag, brought out her slingshot and tucked it in her
pocket. "See you," she said, and jumped to her feet and left
him.

She walked slowly, happy to be alone for a few minutes,
keeping an eye out for small stones for her slingshot, heading
for the next curve in the road to the north, far enough away
from the farmer so that he'd not see her point of entry. She was
thinking what a relief it would be to exchange words with the
farmer after speaking English for these last few hours; news of
the steamer was not her sole purpose in leaving Hamlin, she
knew a deep longing to return to the familiar after being so
quickly wrenched away from Theingyu. Once she reached the
road the farmer saw her and she approached him briskly, think-

ing how he resembled U San Ya just a little, which deepened her pang of homesickness.

She stopped in front of him. *"Nay gaun thlah?"*

He smiled. *"Nay gaun baday,* but I speak English, and you—you are the daughter of the Christian man in Theingyu, the one watched over by a thamma deva?"

She grinned. Of course she and her father had been the only *Amyaji* for a distance of many miles but even if she were Ma Nu herself she knew she would have been quickly placed and identified. "I am, yes," she said, "and I would like to ask if you have seen the steamboat on its way upriver."

He nodded. "I saw, yes."

"Has it passed your village, then?"

"It has passed," he told her, "but I hear that *maneiga*—yesterday—it met with—" He frowned, reaching for the English word. *"Mato tasha?"*

"Accident? What sort of accident, and where?"

He described it with gestures. "It was stuck a long time, long into the night, between—" He named two villages. "It may still be there for I hear the soldiers from the boat were looking for someone."

"How many miles?"

He considered, and held up seven fingers.

Only seven miles away . . . her heart leaped at this news. "Thank you," she said. "Oh thank you very much," she said warmly, and walked back through the rows of stubble, trudged up the road until out of sight and circled back to Hamlin waiting for her on the hill under the neem tree.

"Good news," she told him eagerly. "He says the steamer ran aground yesterday only seven miles from here and may still be there!"

39

"Hey—that *is* good news. That does it, we get moving, daylight or no."

"Not yet," she said as he scrambled to his feet. She rummaged in her bag and brought out her extra shirt, gave it a wistful glance and said, "Sit—I'll make you a *gaumbaun.*" She knelt in front of him, so near that she felt suddenly awkward and self-conscious, aware that Hamlin was not her father, that he was male and she was female, sixteen and nearly a woman, which was another new and strange feeling for her. Frightened that he might sense her confusion she wrenched her gaze away and carefully wrapped the shirt around his head, fashioning it into a turban. However, to observe the effect she quickly moved away from him, a blush lingering warmly on her cheeks. She thought, *This must be what Mi-Mi feels with Chun Tun.*

It was revelation. *"Now* we can go," she told him.

He laughed; he had seen and felt nothing. "How do I look?"

Squinting at him she said in a practical voice, "You might rub some dust across your face to match the dust on your clothes. You're a little tall for a Burmese but your skin is dark enough . . ." She nodded. "From a distance—with the *gaumbaun*—you will look Burmese." She grinned. "But up close they would have to have very bad eyesight to think so."

"Then no one must get near us, obviously!"

They had not watched the fields around them while Gen worked over his *gaumbaun;* now as Hamlin reached to pick up the knapsack he said, "Down! *Get down*—someone's coming!"

Before she flung herself to the ground Gen had a glimpse of one man walking across the field and heading directly toward the hill on which they'd rested. "There is only one," she whispered, watching U Hamlin dig into the knapsack for the knife that was their only weapon.

"Yes but why isn't he on the road? He must have seen us!"

They lay in silence on the warm earth, listening, hearing nothing until a twig snapped nearby and a voice said, "Zen? Zen, it's Ba Tu."

She rolled over and looked up in astonishment at the young man standing over them. "Ba Tu?" she gasped, and to Hamlin, "It's Ma Nu's son!" She leaped to her feet. "How did you find us, where did you come from, I thought you miles away from here in the army!" To U Hamlin she explained, "He's a *sitta,* a soldier."

Hamlin eyed him suspiciously. "Then let him sit down and explain how in hell he knew we were here."

Ba Tu obligingly sat down, and Gen joined him. "I come to return this," he said, reaching into a torn pocket. "I do not know why you are not at home with your father and Ma Nu," he said in a troubled voice, "and I do not know why you walk with this man who is Ingalei," he said, giving Hamlin a hard glance, "but when I saw this I knew you were not in Theingyu."

From his pocket he drew her father's gold watch and dangled it for a moment in the sun before he placed it on the earth between them. "How many times did we play with this, Zen, you and me and Chun Tun and Mi-Mi and Nyun, in the compound of your father?"

Gen looked at the watch, her brows drawn together in a frown. Lifting her eyes to Ba Tu she said slowly, "But I carried this with me when I left Theingyu, Ba Tu, and there is only one place you would have found this watch."

He nodded. "Yes."

"At the pagoda where the dacoits camp."

"Yes."

Hamlin was silent, glancing from one to the other, puzzled, waiting.

She said softly, "It is said in the village you went away to be a soldier. This was not true?"

"No, Zen," he said gravely.

"Then you are the man the dacoits went to meet and bring back to the pagoda for rice?"

"Yes." His eyes began to dance and he grinned boyishly, his teeth very white against his dark face. "And very angry we were to learn there was no money. What a trick you played, Zen, I had to truly laugh when I found the gold watch on the floor of the pagoda and understood what frightened Chi Ti."

"Then you are a dacoit, Ba Tu . . . Oh, what will Ma Nu say?"

"Ma Nu knows."

Gen gasped. "How can that be?"

"Zen," he said seriously, "you know how poor we are, my father works long and hard for U San Ya but without land we will always be poor. This is my chance, I will go back with gold and kyat—already there is some buried deep in the earth back in Theingyu—and when all this fighting is over we will own land at last. You will not speak of this? If the gold watch of your father had not been left behind by mistake in the cave I would not be here, or know how Chi Ti came to be so frightened, but when I saw the gold watch I was troubled. What has happened to take you from Theingyu, Zen?"

Gen told him.

His eyes grew wide, hearing this. When she had finished he said, "But my mother, she doesn't know where you are?"

"There was no time, Ba Tu, and this weighs on my heart a little."

He nodded. "Then I must tell her, for she is worried enough about me and it will go hard with her to worry about you too, Zen." He glanced up at the sun and rose to his feet. "I have to go." He looked at Hamlin and his eyes narrowed. "She is my friend," he said in English, "if any harm comes to her—" He left his warning unspoken but Hamlin understood it very well.

Gen watched Ba Tu stride down the hill, a look of astonishment still lingering on her face. Hamlin said dryly, "You certainly have interesting friends."

"Well, you're a *spy,*" she reminded him crossly.

"How does a person keep names straight in this country? Ba Tu, Ma Nu, San Ya—"

"That's because you don't speak Burmese," she told him. "In English Ba Tu's name would be Mr. Like-his-father."

"I see," he said, blinking, and then, "I hope you'll forgive me if I refer to him then as Like-his-father. Look, that farmer down there must be wondering what the big attraction is up here, we'd better leave before he comes to look. If we hurry we can cover those seven miles in no time at all. Let's go!"

Gathering up knapsack and bag they descended the hill on the side away from the road, cut across a field of partly harvested sesamum and set out north again, walking parallel to the road but keeping it always in sight. They did not speak again until Hamlin guessed they had put six miles behind them, and then they stopped to consider where they were, and to reconnoiter the steamer. Taking cover behind a rise in the ground they looked down on the road and across it to a cluster of roofs enclosed by a bramble fence, its south gate open for the day.

"Know what village that is?" he asked. "Is the river beyond it? What do you think?"

"I don't know, U Hamlin." The sun was warm now and the heat rising, and with it her anxiety. "I can no longer smell the coolness of the river," she told him, "and we've not seen it for more than a mile."

"It has to be there," he said. "I figure if we cross the road just

43

beyond this village, to the north of it, we'll find it again. We must be near the boat now, we've got to be!"

Worried, she said, "But what if the steamer has turned around and started back to Rangoon? I so fear losing it, U Hamlin, I think I must go across the road to the village and ask."

"I couldn't go with you," he reminded her. "Mustn't."

"No—we can meet."

He looked at her closely. "That's what you'd do if you were by yourself?"

When she frankly nodded he realized—and it was humbling —that he was not the protector of this child that he had fancied. He remembered that without him she would have been openly walking—no, bicycling, she'd told him—through every village they'd glimpsed from a distance, perfectly at ease with the inhabitants. Reluctantly accepting her worry he said, "Okay, I'll head north of the village as planned, hide where I can see you leave the village at the other end and we'll meet up there. Are you sure this is a friendly village?"

"You mean insurgents?" she said in surprise. "Oh, they hang a flag when they capture a village and there would be soldiers. You can see how quiet the village is." Giving him a serious glance from the shadows of her hat she added, "But you will watch for me, you will be sure to hide where you can see me?"

"It's a promise."

"Then I'll go now," she announced and stood up, shouldering her bag. He watched her walk over the hill and down to the road before he picked up the knapsack and moved off in the opposite direction.

As for Gen, she walked contentedly, knowing what lay ahead: the village would be mazelike, as hers had been, the lanes and paths overhung by trees and narrowed by high fences made of

44

woven bamboo, slats and woven branches of trees. She knew the cool shadows that fences and trees would throw across the lanes, and that at this hour the women might still be at the village well, drawing water for the day and gossiping, the gates to the compounds open now with children playing, babies asleep in hammocks, a grandmother watching over them, perhaps smoking a huge cheroot like Mi-Mi's grandmother. She walked quickly, anticipation growing in her at seeing this, and of hearing news of the steamboat.

She passed the south gate and the first houses, pausing to marvel at an oleander tree that blazed with color against the monotones of teak and bamboo. Only as she entered the broader lane did it occur to her that the village was strangely quiet, that she was seeing no one at all and hearing neither children nor animals. It was with relief that she caught movement down one of the lanes. A gate had opened and as she stopped to watch she saw a man walk out—no, a soldier, she saw in surprise, a soldier carrying a rifle.

Seeing her his mouth dropped open in astonishment, they eyed each other uncertainly and then as she turned to run away he shouted, *"Hei!"* and lifted his rifle and pointed it at her.

She stopped.

"Bega ladale," he demanded, walking up to her.

"Theingyu," she told him. *"Ba loujindale*—what do you want?"

He was very young and she puzzled him; he peered under her hat into her face and then he walked around her and then he called out to someone, saying there was an Ingalei *meimma* here who spoke Burmese. She was flattered that he described her as a woman but she would have preferred him to lower his rifle. She stood very still and straight, stubbornly refusing fear. She was remembering U Hamlin, hiding by now outside the village and she was thinking how to get away. She thought it might be possible to run from this soldier, who was scarcely older than herself; she did not believe he would shoot her but he would follow, and then what? Seeing her, U Hamlin might shout or wave, come out of hiding, perhaps try to rescue her and then he would be captured, too, and for him it would be dangerous. But seeing the man who strode down the lane to join them her optimism dimmed.

This was a seasoned man of middle age and obviously the leader. He walked with confidence, carrying two eggs in one hand and a rifle in the other. He stopped in front of her and looked her over carefully and it occurred to Gen, staring back at him, that he looked more Chinese than Burmese. Her eyes dropped to the eggs in his hand and she tried not to show her envy.

"Ingalei?" he demanded.

She shook her head. "Ameiyikan."

In English, frowning, he said, "You come from the steamboat?"

This was puzzling. "No, from Theingyu but I am *looking* for the steamer."

This amused him, he laughed and now she was sure that he was not Burmese because he was laughing at her and Burmese never laughed at a person in public, it would have been considered boorish and ill-mannered. "Have you seen the boat?" she asked.

This amused him even more but when he'd finished laughing he lifted his rifle and said, *"Laikkhebala."*

"But I don't *want* to come along," she told him, holding her ground.

"Laikkhebala!" he repeated sharply, and giving over the eggs

46

to his companion he pressed the rifle into her stomach. "Walk!" he told her harshly. *"Checchin*—right away!"

Under her breath she muttered *"Luzou"* and gave him a hostile glance but if he heard her call him a bad man he gave no indication; after all, he had a rifle. Pushing and prodding her from behind he forced her to walk up the lane toward the north gate, his companion following. This was a sad way to send U Hamlin a message that he was in danger and to beware, she thought. They passed the north gate and now at last she saw the river which had made a broad sweep away from the villages and the roads and was returning now to hug the paddies ahead. Beyond the rice fields stood a hill that rose sharply out of the earth to overlook the river, an oddly shaped hill, bald and flattened at the top with dense shrubbery running halfway up its slopes like ragged fur. Her eyes searched the flat field ahead, looking for a rock, a tree where Hamlin might be hiding but unless he had fitted himself into an irrigation ditch she saw nowhere that he might be hiding except in the woods toward which they were heading.

"Where are we going?" she asked. "Where are you taking me?"

"You will see." To the young soldier he said, "She is more *swei* for us, eh, this *nainganjaca?*"

So she was real gold, this "national of a foreign country" but not understanding what this meant she hugged her shoulder bag tightly in case it was her eight hundred kyat of which he spoke, or her father's gold watch.

The river lay tranquil and calm under the late-morning sun, its tranquillity at odds with her feelings, which were growing stormy as she began to understand that she might be denied the steamer now and safe passage to Rangoon. The earth was warm underfoot, the sun intense as they negotiated irrigation ditches

47

and entered the copse of trees in which she was sure that U Hamlin must be hiding. *Oh U Hamlin,* she thought, *we have truly separated now and I am sorry . . . be quiet, be safe!* They passed silently among the trees; she would have liked to look around for signs of U Hamlin but she walked with head averted, eyes on the ground, and presently the earth tilted upward, they had begun to climb the hill through savanna, razor grass and then neem trees—it was a steep hill—and when she reached its bald crown she was gasping. What she saw first, looking to the west, was the great sweep of the Irrawaddy below—the river she had hoped would take her to Rangoon—and then she turned her head and saw that the hill was occupied.

A temple stood on the treeless hilltop, and she guessed a very ancient one from the gaps in its crumbling, faded bricks. It was a small temple with a single broad arched doorway black with shadow under the blazing sun. There were soldiers idling here, half a dozen of them: one sat on the step to the temple, rifle across his lap, while the others stood over a pile of thatch and bricks, scratching their heads and laughing. The laughter broke off when they saw the Man with Two Eggs; they stood at attention and saluted. He nodded to them and pushed Gen toward the temple's doorway and when she hesitated on the threshold he firmly thrust her inside. When she turned around to call him a *luzou* again he had gone, replaced by the guard with his rifle.

Blinded by darkness after the brilliance outside she stood very still, aware of quarrelsome voices from the interior but she could see only vague shapes. The temple held one large square room, cool and dim, each of its walls bearing three high and narrow window-slits through which the brightness of the day outside could be glimpsed without any of its light entering. In the center of the room there rose a massive column of stone into which deep niches had been carved to hold the Buddha images that had long ago been stolen and carried away. The floor was of cool flat paving stones. On the lower interior walls she could see dim, indecipherable scribbles of color that had once been murals before time and vandals had done their work. As her eyes adjusted to the difference in light she began to see more clearly the people standing or sitting against the long wall on her left and she could begin to connect the voices with the people who spoke.

A thin, sour-faced man with a goatee was shouting, "I can't and I won't!"

"I don't think shouting helps."

"Go to hell, I tell you it wasn't my idea to go for a walk."

"Oh dear," murmured a woman's voice.

A large man with untidy hair spoke. "Come now, let us reconcile," and suddenly spying Gen standing in the archway, "Well now, what have we here?"

But Gen was staring at the woman in gray silk who stood against the wall leaning on a cane, the same woman Gen had seen when she had stood on the shore at Theingyu and looked for European faces on the passing steamer.

He would be here too, then, and her glance moved quickly from face to face until she found him in the corner, as she had known that she would: the plump little brown man who had looked at her with recognition from the deck of the boat.

How strange, thought Gen, I have walked into my dream.

5

THE FIGURES UNFROZE, moved, hurled questions at her.

"Where did you come from?"

"Did they free the steamer, are they looking for us?"

"Does anyone know we're here?"

"Did these men tell you who they are? Did they tell you why they captured us?"

"Has the boat left without us?"

"Will there be food soon?"

"Who are you?"

The fierce-looking woman in gray silk stamped her cane. "Stop, all of you!"

But Gen, having listened attentively, said in her clear, precise voice, "Two men brought me here, my name is Gen Ferris, I come from the village of Theingyu, I've been looking for the steamer but I hadn't found it yet, and the man who brought me here had two eggs."

The woman in gray said sharply, "What do you mean, you come from a village here?"

"I live in this country," she said. "In Maymyo and then in Rangoon and lately in Theingyu." She felt no ease in this woman, and she wondered if she was frightened to be so harsh.

"You must speak their language, then! You can find out what these—these bandits—want of us, and tell them we need blankets."

Gen looked at her in surprise. "You wish blankets? Surely *he* speaks Burmese," she said, pointing toward the plump brown-faced man in the corner.

"No doubt, but scarcely English," the woman said dismissingly.

"But I think he does speak English," Gen said with a knowledge that surprised her. "You do, don't you?"

He bowed slightly, looking amused, and in accentless English said, "I speak English, yes."

An awkward and embarrassed silence followed this, during which the woman in gray glared at Gen before reluctantly turning to the Burmese. "How do you happen to be with us?" she inquired coldly.

He shrugged. "I too felt that a walk would be most beneficial while waiting for the steamer to be freed."

"You were on the steamer, then?" Her voice was sharp.

"You don't suppose he led us into that trap, do you?" said the goateed man nastily.

"Oh he couldn't have," burst out a shy, plain-looking woman. "I mean, he walked *behind* us, he walked behind *me,* so he couldn't have led us into *anything.*" Immediately she looked chagrined at her boldness.

51

"How did it happen?" Gen asked of this softer woman.

"Oh, we saw the village in the distance and decided to visit it," she said eagerly, "except suddenly these men surrounded us. They came out of the woods before we even reached the village."

"Ruffians," snorted the woman in gray silk.

"No no, not ruffians," said the Burmese politely. "Soldiers— members of the Red Flag Army."

"Army? Nonsense, how do you know this?"

"You did not notice the red arm bands?"

Gen, puzzled, told him, "I feel as if I know you but I don't know your name."

His brown eyes twinkled at her. "I am Mr. Ba Sein, address number 16, Jubaliho Street, Rangoon."

"And I'm Mrs. Harry Caswell," said the shy woman eagerly. "Or Helen," she added with an air of surprise.

"Enough!" cried the woman with the cane. "If you know who our captors are then perhaps," she said icily, "you also know what they plan for us; you must surely have heard something?"

Gen was now sure that this woman was a *balu,* an ogre.

"From what I overheard," responded U Ba Sein calmly, "they have teletyped a message to Rangoon, to the Prime Minister U Nu, telling him they hold five Europeans here and offering to negotiate for release."

"Why didn't you tell us this before?" she demanded.

He bowed ever so slightly. "I felt it would have been most forward of me to intrude without invitation."

"You British with your subject people," muttered the large man with wildly untidy hair.

"Come now," said the thin man with the goatee, "perhaps Lady Waring did not realize, did not notice, did not see—"

"Lady?" repeated Gen, puzzled. "Oh but ladies—surely ladies aren't so rude?"

"I *beg* your pardon!" said Lady Waring, taken aback.

"Well, yes," said Gen. "Like a balu." But these people and their conversation had ceased to interest her and she turned away, determined to escape as quickly as possible and return to U Hamlin.

Her remark had been followed by a stricken silence, interrupted now by a chuckle from the large man with untidy hair. "Permit me to introduce us all," he said. "I myself am Terence Baharian, a wild Armenian now a citizen of the United States. The senior member of our little party—a strange word for this unhappy gathering—is, as you have heard, Lady Waring. The gentleman next to her is Mr. Gunfer, who tells us that he is a writer of travel books and had planned to make known this exotic country to his readers. Mrs. Caswell has already introduced herself. There is one more of us but she is asleep behind this—this chimney or whatever it is."

"It's not a chimney, it's for the Buddha images," Gen said, and removing her shoulder bag she placed it against the wall and walked to the arched doorway to look outside. She was worried about U Hamlin, worried that he might have been found by the soldiers and shot; she hoped ardently that he was still free and yet half hoped, too, that he might be found and brought here so that she could see him again, for certainly he was much pleasanter than the noisy Europeans inside the temple who were strange to her.

There were four soldiers outside now, three of them laying thatch over a guard house they'd built of bamboo and the bricks that had fallen from the temple. The fourth, watching her, lifted his rifle.

She sat down on the step in the sun and called to him, *"Zaga takhun hnakhun pyojinde*—I'd like to have a word with you!"

He strolled closer, rifle cradled under his arm, and she told him the people inside needed blankets for the night. "Can you find blankets? If they are important people," she reminded him, "you don't want them to get sick."

"Watch out or I'll steal your hat," he teased.

"If you steal my hat I will tell the balu who is inside to put a spell on you," she said sternly. "And she is a real balu."

"This I can believe, I have seen and heard her," he said, grinning. "And she needs a *saun?"*

"Six are needed—*hcau.* Can you find blankets?"

There would be blankets in the village below, he said but when she asked where the people of the village had gone he only shook his head and walked away, calling over his shoulder that some blankets would be brought with their *thamin,* cooked rice.

Gen lingered, examining this clumsy arrangement to guard them, thinking how when night came she could easily slip out of the temple and disappear into the darkness. The eight hundred kyat, rescued after all, were in her shoulder bag; if she found the steamer she might find U Hamlin again, for surely if he'd not been captured he would continue north looking for it rather than face walking the long miles south to Rangoon.

She sighed, for the day that had begun so well had lost all its promise. She stared unseeingly at the sunbaked golden earth and then her gaze lengthened to include the wide sweep of river below. Immediately in front of her its passage was obscured by the hill on which the temple was built and by a screen of palms and bamboo groves, but the river appeared again to the north and for a moment she forgot entrapment, imagining the river flowing steadily toward the steamer, upriver. She sighed again, impatient for the darkness that would free her, and reluctantly went back inside.

"Ah here she is," cried the jovial Baharian as she reappeared. "Did I not tell you, Miss Thorald, we have been joined by another while you slept?"

"I was tired," Miss Thorald said vaguely, and turned an intense gaze on Gen that belied any tiredness, and at once plunged Gen's spirits deeper. At this moment Gen was passionately and ardently glad that U Hamlin was not with her because she thought Miss Thorald more beautiful than anyone she had seen, more beautiful than any of the movie stars she had pinned to her wall in Theingyu. Her hair was the color of ripe apricots, and in spite of being severely pulled into a knot, all kinds of curls and waves and ringlets escaped. And the face—Gen was humbled: it was small and perfectly oval with high cheekbones and sloe eyes heavily fringed with lashes. Lady Waring might have thought Miss Thorald pretty but it was Gen who recognized the passion in that face, not understanding that it reflected the passion inside of herself, as yet unmined.

Gen said formally, "How do you do," and to Lady Waring, "They will bring blankets with the rice."

"The little one is efficient as well!" boomed Baharian.

Miss Thorald said to Gen softly, "I'm told that you've lived in Burma all your life and I hope you'll tell me what it's like . . . perhaps you can also teach me a few words of Burmese."

"You?" said Gen, surprised. "Where are you going?"

She said simply, "To live with my brother who's a missionary up near a place called Lashio."

Her voice had been soft but it was heard and it produced reaction.

"Oh my dear, why?" said Helen Caswell in a shocked voice.

"You're much too young and pretty to hide yourself away like that, surely?"

Miss Thorald's smile was ironic. "Indeed?"

Baharian stared at her with open curiosity. "But this is extraordinary waste that breaks the heart! Are you religiously inclined, then?"

Gen, watching her, said, "My father was a missionary."

"Then perhaps," said Miss Thorald lightly, "you can tell me about that, too." Seating herself on the floor, her back to the wall, she opened a small petit point bag, brought out wool and needles and began to knit, very firmly ending the conversation but leaving everyone regarding her with curiosity.

"Well now," said Baharian, hands in pocket and surveying them all with interest, "the Miss Thorald goes to a brother— and you, Mrs. Caswell? It will pass the time, I am thinking, to learn why we are all here. In this land."

"Oh, I'm with my husband," Helen Caswell said quickly. "He's an archaeologist, you see, and we've been given permission by the Director of Archaeological Survey to investigate rumors of cave paintings in the north. He's a very *well-known* archaeologist," she added firmly.

"We know that Mr. Gunfer is a travel writer—he has said so often enough," went on Baharian, "but dare we ask, Lady Waring, why you venture into these wilds?"

"I find you impertinent, Mr. Baharian," said Lady Waring.

"But of course! I agree most heartily. Perhaps no one has been impertinent before?"

"That child is impertinent," she said stiffly. "I may perhaps ask what a balu is?"

"Oh, an ogre," said Gen.

Lady Waring's lips tightened. Baharian laughed. Miss Thorald glanced quickly from him to Lady Waring and returned to her knitting. Both Gunfer and Mrs. Caswell looked shocked.

"My business here," said Lady Waring gruffly, "is my own business. And you, Mr. Baharian? Is your business your own, too? I would guess you to be an adventurer of the very worst sort."

"An adventurer, yes," he assured her gravely, "but not of the worst sort, please! I am here to hunt for treasure in the most *respectable* manner."

"Treasure!" echoed Mr. Gunfer. "You're pulling our legs, surely!"

"I would not dare," said Baharian gravely. "No, it is a most interesting story but only to me. Half of my family emigrated to America, half to England. My uncle chose England and then Burma, where he bought land and had a farm of many acres and lived a most pleasant life until the war. When the Japanese came he fled to India, carrying with him no more than a few gold coins for survival. The rest of his riches he left buried in the earth—but I will not tell you where—and he has commissioned me, his nephew, Terence P. Baharian, to recover his treasure."

Lady Waring said dryly, "And if your story is true, then just how do you expect to get this treasure out of the country? Rangoon appears to be extremely suspicious of Europeans."

Baharian beamed at her happily. "Ah but there will be a way, Lady Waring, and then—voilà!—I may yet become the adventurer you think me."

"I don't believe you," sniffed Lady Waring. "I don't believe any uncle would entrust you with such matters."

Baharian made a sweeping bow. "A little mystery suits me well, then, if that's what you prefer. And you, small one?" he asked, turning to Gen.

She said, "My father—" She stopped; she would not be

among them for long and she saw no reason to confide in them. "I'm being sent to Rangoon," she said, "but the steamer didn't stop at our village and so I set out to find it."

"Sent to Rangoon *alone?*" gasped Mrs. Caswell.

Gen hesitated and then smiled. "No, I was accompanied but now we've been separated. By this," she added.

Baharian nodded; her fabrication was accepted. "And you, Mr.—is it Ba Sein?"

U Ba Sein considered a moment. "I have come this way to meet someone," he said.

"And what do you do at number 16 Jubaliho Street in Rangoon?"

Mr. Ba Sein smiled faintly. "I am a puppetmaster. My theater, called the Jubaliho, also lives at number 16 Jubaliho in Rangoon."

Gen turned white with excitement. "Truly? A puppetmaster?" She rushed to her shoulder bag and carried it to him. "Look," she said, eagerly extracting her marionette. "Htun Schwae carved and made this for me, he traveled many years ago with a troupe."

Ba Sein took it reverently. "Zawgwi," he murmured, his eyes running over it with satisfaction.

"What a darling puppet," said Miss Thorald.

"Magnificent," breathed Mrs. Caswell.

Mr. Gunfer left Lady Waring's side to look at it. "Who is it? You called it by name?"

"The alchemist with powers of magic and necromancy, Zawgwi," murmured U Ba Sein. "A demigod who can fly through the air or tunnel through the earth with his magic powers." Holding it up he examined its eight strings and rose to his feet, fingers holding the bar. Moving the strings the puppet suddenly took a few steps, bowed, turned his head, pointed a hand at Gen, opened his mouth and closed it.

"Oh, could you show me how to do that?" cried Gen. "You made him as alive as any of us!"

"Puppets *are* alive," he told her. "Your Zawgwi is small, with only eight strings, but he was carved with love, and beautifully."

"Yes," agreed Gen. "But still, with only eight strings—there should be more?"

"The marionettes of my theater have as many as twenty, twenty-six," he told her, gently returning the marionette to her. "Yes, I can show you how to make him live, even with eight strings. If you wish."

"I do wish," she told him fervently. "Oh I do wish, yes." She looked with new eyes at Zawgwi, did not return him to the shoulder bag but began exploring the strings and the movements as she had often done before but without the art of Mr. Ba Sein. A glow of excitement had taken her unaware; like the puppet in the hands of U Ba Sein she felt stirred by aliveness. "When can we start?" she asked, forgetting the open doorway and the coming night.

But Lady Waring interrupted. "We begin to need water to drink, Mr.—er—"

Mrs. Caswell nodded eagerly. "Yes indeed, the air is certainly dry in Burma, isn't it. But surely we won't be here long?"

U Ba Sein looked at her in surprise. "Why will we not?"

"You said a message had been sent—"

He padded to the doorway without reply. "I will ask what arrangements they make for drinking water." His plump body was momentarily silhouetted against the brilliant sun outside, he called *"Hei"* and disappeared.

Baharian said, "I think he's trying to tell us that government troops may not be in the neighborhood."

"Nonsense," said Lady Waring, "if they're fighting in Mandalay that's not far!"

"They may not be fighting in Mandalay."

"They could send planes, then."

"I'm told there are only three planes in the country."

"Enough to bring soldiers to free us!"

Mrs. Caswell said anxiously, "But there were government soldiers traveling with us on the steamer, and *they* must surely be looking for us and not far away! My husband must be frantic, he'd never allow them to just—just go on."

"Nor Mr. Culpepper," added Lady Waring. "He was specifically assigned to me by the Consul in Rangoon."

U Ba Sein reappeared in the doorway to say, "They are digging a latrine at this moment, a deep hole in the ground to the left of the doorway. For water, the guard will inquire instructions of his superior."

"But how long—" Lady Waring bit her lip. "Did you learn their plans?"

U Ba Sein said cheerfully, "Only that they appear to find us of much value to their plans, which remain unspoken."

"Will they harm us?" asked Mrs. Caswell anxiously.

"They wouldn't dare," said Lady Waring. "They noted down all our names and passport numbers last night and surely must have sent them to Rangoon along with whatever they want in exchange for us. The British may have turned the country over to these—these people—two years ago but the British *cannot* be without influence and the name of Waring won't be ignored, the Consul will see to that."

Gen, who had been listening politely and considering what Mr. Ba Sein had just said, spoke what to her seemed an obvious truth. "If they are digging a latrine they must expect to be here a long time."

"Tactless child," said Baharian lightly. "If that should be the case—of course we cannot know—perhaps we would be very clever to make housing arrangements, and a few rules."

"Quite unnecessary," said Lady Waring flatly.

"Like what?" asked Gen with interest.

But no one could think of any rules or arrangements, or did not want to, and the conversation subsided, Mrs. Caswell withdrawing behind the pillar for a nap, the day's heat penetrating even the cool walls of the temple and rendering them listless.

There was no midday food. Hungry, angry and craving freedom, Gen fled to the step of the temple where she could sit and think about her escape route, given only fleeting glances by the two guards who were engaged in a game of dominoes. Hugging her knees and considering her plans she could foresee no problem for a single person slipping away into the darkness: one minute the guards would see her sitting in the doorway, the next moment she would have vanished but it would be assumed that she had gone inside to join the others. If not, a few shots might be fired but she could run fast, and once down the hill she would need only a few trees to hide herself in the night. The only problem, as she saw it, lay in which direction to head to avoid more soldiers and she was wondering if somehow she might gain information from the guards when U Ba Sein walked through the archway and sat down beside her.

"I have brought your Zawgwi," he said.

She turned her head, and finding him so near she looked closely into his face in the sunlight: at the high broad forehead, the short blunt nose, the line that curved down from each side of his nose to divide his plump cheeks from the full-lipped mouth and round chin.

"I will show you something," he said. "I will show you how one starts to bring a puppet to life."

He had captured her attention and Gen waited.

Holding up the marionette he said gravely, "First we must ask Zawgwi to please not be offended if we change him—not for long—into others. Now," he said to Gen, "who among those in the temple walks like this?"

His fingers moved among the strings and Zawgwi's red wand dropped, turned vertical until it touched the ground and tapped angrily up and down; Gen laughed in spite of herself. "It is the lady in gray silk with the cane, called Lady Someone."

"Yes . . . now what of U Baharian, how does he walk?"

"U Ba Sein, I came only this morning!" she protested.

"But one must observe, observe!" he told her. "Describe this Mr. Baharian to me as you remember him."

"He's very large," she said, considering this. "He looks like a wild man with his hair like a bird's nest but his face is round and jolly and it shines . . . He stood often with hands on his hips . . . Yes, like that," she said, smiling as U Ba Sein illustrated each word with a lift of the rod and a twitch of the strings.

"Very good," he said. "And Miss Thorald?"

Gen turned wistful. "She's very beautiful, she'd walk like the princess in the Creation of the World."

U Ba Sein's fingers moved deftly and the puppet walked with grace. "And Mrs. Caswell?"

"She is the other lady? She would walk with apology, U Ba Sein, her shoulders drooping—so." And as she dropped her shoulders so did the marionette, so perfectly that Gen laughed.

"And Mr. Gunfer?"

"Oh he is very sour," she told him. "He moves stiffly, as if his joints need sesamum oil."

It was U Ba Sein who laughed now. "Very very good, Zen,

62

you have seen more than you realize. To quote the English Shakespeare, 'All the world's a stage and all the men and women merely players.' To bring these little people to life they must speak, walk, gesture like humans, until they become the very shadows and reflections of human people. And the puppetmaster—it is the puppetmaster who moves them, just as kan —destiny—moves us." He gave her an interested glance. "You are planning—thinking of—leaving us?"

Startled by his reading of her thoughts she said, "I don't like being a prisoner, U Ba Sein."

"But we are all prisoners from birth to death," he said softly. "You will learn this."

Puzzled, she said, "What does that mean?"

"That is for you to discover." Standing up he stretched out a hand to her. "Come—come inside, there is a feast of people in there to observe, and if you are serious to learn—"

"I am, U Ba Sein," she said, and followed him inside.

Near sunset time the soldiers brought them blankets, two wooden buckets filled with water, three candles, matches and a kettle of rice.

The rice was cold and glutinous and it was the only food they brought. The blankets had holes in them. A drowned grasshopper floated in one of the pails of water.

And when they had delivered food and blankets they shattered all of Gen's plans for escape in the darkness: they brought up from the village a huge wooden gate which they nailed over the arched doorway, closing them in for the night.

6

GEN SLEPT BADLY, feeling caged and nearly suffocated by the nearness of the others. Waking frequently it was to hear the same sounds that she'd heard in Rangoon during the war: snores, small groans as bodies turned on the hard stone floor, coughs, the footsteps of the sentries outside. And it was cold.

The gate was removed just before dawn, and Mr. Ba Sein and Baharian summoned to go to the river and bring up water, accompanied by guards. Hearing this, Lady Waring cried out, "The water comes from the river? Good God, tell them we must have our water boiled or we'll all come down with dysentery!"

Mr. Gunfer's head appeared turtlelike from under his blanket. "The thought of another day here absolutely appalls me," he announced. "There has to be something we can do to get out of here before we all die of boredom or starvation."

"Much of Asia lives on rice," Mrs. Caswell told him reproachfully. "And if you're suggesting escape—" Her glance moved pointedly to Lady Waring.

"I can walk," snapped Lady Waring. "Of course I can walk, I walked up this hill, didn't I?"

"But your cane—"

Lady Waring gave her a sardonic glance. "This cane of mine is sheer affectation. It pleases me to use it, I'm a very infractious and insubordinate old woman and do not go kindly into the night."

"How old *are* you?" asked Gen.

"Hear the child! Tactless again but I'm sixty-eight."

"My goodness that's not old," Gen told her. "U Htun Schwae is seventy-six, which is much older—although of course he's a very happy person."

"Fortunate man," said Lady Waring dryly, and meeting tactlessness with tactlessness, "I prefer to make people *un*happy. A cane helps, I can stamp it on the ground, trip people up, rap them lightly on the legs—as my secretary Moreland can attest—and in general get far more attention. But I can walk, thank you. Tell them, Mr. Ba Sein, we must have boiled water," and with a defiant glance at Mrs. Caswell she added, "and you might also count how many soldiers you see in case we decide to escape."

This last suggestion pleased Gen; she followed the men to the doorway and sat on the brick step in the cool fresh air to watch them go, U Ba Sein and Baharian each carrying a bucket, the two guards their rifles, the figures growing smaller and then dropping behind the hill that led to the river. It was a steep hill and Gen thought that it would go hard with them to bring up filled buckets. She received a few furtive glances from the remaining sentry, who was mixing areca, lime and tobacco on a palm leaf. She wondered where U Hamlin might be in this first dawn since they'd been separated; he was not spoiled and soft like these people, she thought, and she wondered how many soldiers U Ba Sein would count so that she could make new plans to get away. How easy it would be, for instance, to walk away right now, she thought, with no barricade and only one guard. What held her back was her lack of information, for she was remembering with disapproval how naively she had strolled into the village below the hill yesterday, never dreaming she would meet with soldiers. Obviously there was more to be understood and observed before any new attempt could be planned. It was a matter of examining her kan and of hoping for guidance from her thamma deva.

Her gaze moved beyond the sentry to the erupting color in the east and a sky laced with marvels of color. The fragrances of damp earth and of jasmine drifted to her on the air and she sniffed appreciatively after the stale night air in the temple. Later the breeze would falter and the sun rule a cloudless sky but the sun's rise was still moments away, and with it came the hush of expectation.

She felt someone behind her and Lady Waring moved to sit down at the opposite end of the step. "I need to warm my bones," she said, and with a glance at Gen, "I won't bite."

Gen said nothing, for the sun was appearing now—a huge and fiery globe—as it would appear day after day until the end of time, and this constancy was of comfort to her just now as she watched the mist over the Irrawaddy begin to retreat into the shadows under the hills, leaving the river a stream of gold.

" 'Where the dawn comes up like thunder,' " murmured Lady Waring. She turned and looked at Gen. "You know, you are quite as rude as I am, but at your age you should make an attempt to please, it's considered proper." She was silent, considering this. "Although not like Mrs. Caswell, of course."

"Mrs. Caswell?" Gen brought herself back to the moment and tried to remember who Mrs. Caswell was.

"A dithery sort of woman," continued Lady Waring. "One could observe this on the steamer. A self-important husband who has rendered her totally helpless as to who she is, a very definite example of why I dislike women."

Gen turned and looked at her curiously.

"Oh yes," said Lady Waring. "Poor spineless creatures in general."

"Miss Thorald, too?"

Lady Waring sniffed. "Time will tell. I don't understand why you're going to Rangoon at such an indecent time," she said. "Your parents must be insane to allow it."

Gen said frankly, "I don't understand why you're here either, traveling north in this country."

Lady Waring looked at her with exasperation. "You're supposed to properly answer questions and try to please your elders, young woman, and above all not be impertinent. As to why I'm here, I keep my grief to myself, thank you."

"Grief?" said Gen, suddenly stilled. "Grief?"

Lady Waring, surprised by this arresting of motion, this involuntary stillness in the girl, gave her a long and thoughtful glance. Something in Gen's voice, in her face, moved her to say gruffly, against her will, "My son is buried in this country."

Gen looked at her questioningly.

"He was a glider pilot," said Lady Waring stiffly. "In the RAF. They called the planes 'whispering death' and death it brought him. I intend—will and *must*," she emphasized grimly, "bring him back to England for proper burial."

"How will you find his grave?" Gen asked in a practical voice.

Lady Waring's lips tightened. "I have spent a great deal of time searching for the survivors of that mission behind Japanese lines in '44. I have the name of the village in Upper Burma written down very carefully, and a map of where they buried the twenty-three men who crashed, and I have made a *great* deal of trouble for a great many people to get here. He was only twenty-two when he died. And he was my *son,"* she added.

There were tears in her eyes and Gen, seeing this, thought that perhaps she was not, after all, a balu. If this was confusing to her it brought with it the thought that perhaps Europeans wore masks to hide themselves. This possibility answered a great puzzle in her; it might explain, for instance, whatever unseen despairs had gripped her father when he chose to end his life, for he had smiled at her only that morning, if somewhat absently, just as he had smiled at her every morning over their breakfast rice. The idea was new but interesting, if untested, for the only masks worn among the Burmese were masks of courtesy and of great tact; they had brought to an art the principle of never saying no, and carefully avoided placing anyone else in a position to say no. Lady Waring's hiding of herself was different, Gen decided, not recognizing her own mask, and if she was to live among such people this was something she must study and observe. It was possible their skins were only shells, like a nut, and if the shell was broken there would be fruit inside, although at the moment they seemed more like stones to her, polished and impervious, with no meat inside.

"What was his name?" she asked.

"Eric."

A name made this dead son more real, and thinking about

this Gen's thoughts convulsed and formed into expressible words. She asked, "Is life nothing except loss?"

Behind them Mr. Gunfer said, "What a bizarre display of color, I had no idea Nature could be so vulgar, just look!"

"I *am* looking," snapped Lady Waring, annoyed by his interruption. "If you observe carefully you will see that I sit facing the sunrise and would have to be utterly myopic to miss it, and vulgarity, Mr. Gunfer, is in the eye of the beholder. Help me up," she added peevishly. "I don't like change, I miss my toothbrush, a night's sleep in a bed, and I dare not even consider breakfast but at least I can comb my hair."

Impervious to her hostility Mr. Gunfer extended his hand. "Today we really *must* insist on firewood to boil our water, Lady Waring."

She nodded and pointed her cane at Gen. "You," she said. "You or whatever-his-name-is—speak to a guard about it."

"His name is Mr. Ba Sein," pointed out Gen. "It means diamond."

"In the rough?" cackled Mr. Gunfer, and guided Lady Waring inside.

As the colors in the sky rearranged themselves into a simple golden radiance that might have pleased even Mr. Gunfer, four heads came into view over the rim of the hill, reached the crest and stopped while Baharian put down his pail to wipe his forehead with his sleeve. When they resumed walking Gen stood up to greet them. She asked softly, "Were there soldiers?"

U Ba Sein answered. "I counted twelve foreheads bathing in the river."

She nodded. "It's that time of day, yes. Next time I will take a turn at going for water and see."

"And a thirteenth soldier guarding them and their rifles on the shore," added U Ba Sein sternly, and went inside.

69

After considering this depressing news for a few minutes Gen followed them inside to hear Baharian say, "Very interesting! I like the dramatic idea myself but it is scarcely to the point to speak of escape if there are a dozen soldiers bathing, and who knows how many other soldiers in the neighborhood. Me, I would not enjoy using great guile and cunning against the guards—not to mention Lady Waring's cane," he added with a bow to her, "only to reach the base of the hill and be caught all over again."

Miss Thorald said, "Perhaps we should postpone speaking of this until tomorrow."

"It's going to be another long night," sighed Mrs. Caswell. "And I'm so *hungry.*"

Gen suggested grasshoppers. "If we could catch some—like the one that was floating in the water pail, only fresh—"

She was regarded with astonishment. "What would we do with grasshoppers?"

"They're a wonderful treat when fried."

"Good God!" said Gunfer.

"Revolting," murmured Lady Waring.

Only Mrs. Caswell was unmoved and looked at Gen with interest. "I suppose you know a great great deal about this country, its customs and beliefs."

Gen said vaguely, "I suppose."

"Do you know as much about America?"

She shook her head. "Except that its President is Harold Truman."

"*Harry* Truman," said Lady Waring.

"Would you consider removing your hat?" suggested Baharian in a kind voice. "You interest me, small one. Anyone who recommends grasshoppers—would they be considered en-

70

trée or appetizer?—interests me deeply. What do you look like under that hat, can we persuade you to remove it?"

Responding to the kindness in his voice Gen reached up and removed her hat.

"Good God, she has hair," said Mr. Gunfer.

"Indeed yes, and look at those eyes." Baharian spoke with such exaggerated drama that Gen laughed. "Green as a cat's eyes—lovely!"

"Really?" said Gen, touched and surprised, having not been given such attention for a long time. "But I don't have breasts yet."

Baharian laughed, Mr. Gunfer snickered and Lady Waring gave her a sharp glance. "There is no need to speak of such things," she told her.

"But it's the truth," protested Gen.

"To speak such truth is rude, you have to *change!*"

Gen said defiantly, "I thought you didn't like change."

"There you go again," said Lady Waring. "You're bad for my blood pressure, go away."

"She means you give as good as you get, you outsmart her," Baharian said, beaming at Gen. "Truth does that—kindly do *not* change."

Gen thought about this. "I think I'd prefer people to like me."

"Then you'll never be free, small one, don't you know that? Be yourself."

U Hamlin had said this, too, although humorously and not without some malice, she remembered. It all seemed very difficult, meeting these people from another world, and she sighed.

Miss Thorald glanced up from her knitting and said tactfully, "It's true that she's unusual but her hair needs a trim. I could do this with my sewing scissors if she'd allow it."

71

"Will I look more American?" asked Gen.

"Listen!" interrupted U Ba Sein, holding up one hand to still them.

They were silent, hearing the sound of guns firing below the hill. The rifle fire was sharp, staccato and sounded surprisingly close to them as it stopped, began again, stopped, resumed.

Baharian said dryly, "They are no longer bathing in the river."

Gen closed her eyes and prayed to her father's God that they'd not found U Hamlin.

The exchange of fire moved away, shrank in volume, became distant and then died, but there was no more talk of escape, and they turned almost gratefully to a discussion of Gen's hair. "Because," said Baharian, "I think we very much need the diversion now of that promised haircut by the beautiful Miss Thorald who owns our only pair of scissors. You are prepared, small one?"

"Yes," Gen said, and fumbled eagerly in her shoulder bag for her magazine. "Can I look like one of *them?* I don't have curls," she said, shyly handing the precious magazine to Miss Thorald. "They all have curls and fringes."

"They're called 'bangs,' not fringes," Mrs. Caswell said, peering over Miss Thorald's shoulder.

"Insipid," said Lady Waring, craning her neck to see. "Make her look like a doll."

"Then I'll give her a side part and comb it nicely across the brow, and merely trim the ends."

"I'd rather have bangs," Gen said stubbornly.

Baharian said, "What interests me more than bangs is what each of us has brought here. The small one's bag reminds me: from it she pulls a marionette called Zawgwi and now a magazine. Miss Thorald has brought with her the knitting bag in which she carries wool and scissors. I would suggest we empty our pockets to learn what other treasures we have to fortify us."

Mr. Gunfer said explosively, "A violation of privacy, Baharian!"

"For myself," said Baharian, ignoring him, "I place on the floor a paperback copy of Shaw's *The Young Lions,* my passport and my wallet. Miss Thorald?"

She had brought out her scissors; a razor blade fell to the floor and she hastily picked it up, stuffing it back in the knitting bag, her face scarlet. "Besides my knitting and scissors I have one paperback book and a small hardcover book. You want them on the floor, too?"

Mrs. Caswell said eagerly, "Oh please yes, I love a good read, we'll have a library!"

The two books were placed on the floor and Baharian looked at their titles and then at Miss Thorald. *"The Wisdom of Lao-tse—* and essays of Emerson?" he said softly.

Miss Thorald said nothing.

"Not novels," Mrs. Caswell said, disappointed.

"Well, I have nothing except my passport," sniffed Lady Waring, "and a small bottle of aspirin."

"Which may prove of infinite value . . . And you, Mr. Ba Sein?"

He bowed and brought from the folds of his longyi a carving tool with a wooden handle, a pencil, a small notebook and a pair of reading glasses.

"And you, small one?"

Gen removed the contents of her shoulder bag piece by piece and placed them on the floor: the slingshot, the eight hundred kyat, the knife and matches, the child's book of crossword puzzles—used over and over by erasing each penciled entry—the passport and her birth certificate. There was still a small bulge when she felt inside, and to her surprise she found the little bag of tea that had started out in the knapsack. "Tea!" she said, pleased.

"Bravo," commented Baharian, and turned to Mr. Gunfer.

"Oh no," said Gunfer, backing away.

"Oh yes," said Baharian. "I'm twice your size, Mr. Gunfer, I warn you I shall—*what are you hiding?*"

"You wouldn't dare!"

Baharian seized him and gripped both of his arms. "Lady Waring, kindly see what Mr. Gunfer is going to voluntarily and graciously offer to share with us, eh?"

Lady Waring, looking amused, moved to empty his pockets while Gunfer protested vehemently. Her look of amusement faded as she lifted two chocolate bars from his left pocket. "Chocolate!" she cried indignantly. "And all of us so hungry? Shame on you, Mr. Gunfer!"

"Shame!" he shouted at her. "What about the pearl necklace I saw you slide inside your dress when they captured us? Worth a king's ransom, I'd guess. What about that, you haven't mentioned that, have you?"

Mrs. Caswell, covering her ears, cried, "Oh stop, I can't bear shouting!"

"That's *your* problem," Lady Waring told her angrily, and to Mr. Gunfer, "My pearls are of great sentimental value to me and I need not point out that they're scarcely *edible.* If you're thinking I could use them as a bribe to get us out of here, don't be a fool, these people are fanatics and politicians, they'd only accept the pearls and laugh at us. They much prefer to humiliate us." Reaching into his other pocket she angrily removed a paperback book with a lurid cover. "And here's a novel for you, Mrs. Caswell," she said contemptuously. *"Vampire Love* by Cynthia Gore, author of—it says here—*Mrs. Carlisle's Folly* and

Blood on the Moon. What strange taste you have in reading, Mr. Gunfer!"

"Thank you," said Mrs. Caswell, apparently unaware of her contempt and looking pleased. "I read *Blood on the Moon* in— yes, it was when we were in Egypt."

Mr. Gunfer regarded her with hatred before turning back to Baharian. "You will unleash me now, please, after this—this rape. Thieves, all of you—those were my chocolate bars, mine!"

"Let's not get hysterical," said Baharian.

Ignoring the storm around them Miss Thorald knelt beside Gen, scissors in hand. "I'll give you bangs," she whispered with a conspiratorial smile, her face so near to Gen that she could see just how she might carve her features in wood, if given the chance to carve a princess. She studied the slant of the high cheekbones, the small heart-shaped mouth, the eyes that subtly tilted at their outer corners, and then as Miss Thorald lifted her scissors Gen forgot puppets and gave herself up to the bliss of being redesigned.

7

LADY WARING thought Gen's haircut dreadful but she held her tongue. She was curious about the girl—a child emotionally, she felt, yet oddly adult in so many ways—and forgetting how she herself had been at sixteen these contradictions challenged her. At least the girl was not cut from the common pattern, she decided, thinking of her own two daughters whom she disliked intensely. The girl carried secrets and Lady Waring, being well acquainted with secrets, looked forward to ferreting them out of her, it would give her something to do—that is, if she could wrest the girl away from Mr. Ba Sein; at the moment the two were seated on the step in the doorway and he was demonstrating with pencil and notebook how to plan the carving of a marionette's head. She sighed; the stone floor was cold and hard and with an effort she stood up, quelling with a glance Mrs. Caswell's move to help her. ("You don't suffer fools lightly," Matthew had said once, to which she had replied, "Would you, if you were surrounded by them?") Mrs. Caswell had returned to her reading of that dreadful book *Vampire Love,* Miss Thorald was knitting, Mr. Gunfer staring gloomily at the walls, and Baharian was pacing. "Ten times around the pillar I shall call one lap," he had announced. "I am a large man, I need exercise." Mr. Gunfer had been right about boredom, thought Lady Waring, she might very well die of it closeted here with these impossible people while waiting for her trip north to continue. Of them all, she found Mr. Gunfer the most distasteful, he had actually turned vicious about the pearls she now wore tucked inside her blouse. But no one—*no one,* she thought fiercely—was going to take away her pearls, they were all that she had of her son Eric, they had been his gift to her on the day that he'd reached his majority and received his inheritance, presented to her with a bow and that bewitching smile of his—*but I mustn't think of Eric,* she thought, and she walked across the room to peer at the faded designs on the wall, at eroded figures of men in robes, a nearly indecipherable collection of temples and the faded head of a Buddha. She would ask Gen or Mr. Ba Sein about these, she decided, it would give her something to think about.

The quiet was interrupted by Gen rushing in to say, "The Man with Two Eggs is coming."

"Who?"

"The man who captured me in the village below the hill, I think he's an officer."

Baharian stopped pacing, Miss Thorald looked up from her knitting, Mrs. Caswell rose nervously to her feet, Mr. Gunfer said petulantly, "It's high time we receive attention from a superior."

The man who entered introduced himself curtly as Colonel

Wang. A peasant colonel, mused Lady Waring, studying his rough-featured face, but an efficient and ambitious-looking man, and therefore dangerous. Obviously he was in a hurry, impatient at this need to stop and see them. He said testily, "You have blankets and now I hear you ask for *wood?*"

He had addressed Baharian and it was Baharian who replied. "Firewood. We're all very thirsty but dare not drink water from the river."

Lady Waring added coldly, "You might add that we'll soon die of starvation as well, if that's what he wants."

"One thing at a time," Baharian told her firmly, and to Colonel Wang, "We'd like to boil our drinking water."

"Ah yes, I see," he said, and nodded. "Very well—that can be done."

"We heard guns," said Mrs. Caswell timidly.

"Yes," he said. "Some fools thought they could take back the village below."

"What village is it?" asked Baharian.

"It's called Badamyâ." He looked them all over, nodded and strode out.

Lady Waring followed him. "Colonel Wang!" she said sharply.

He stopped under the archway and turned. "Yes?"

"As the eldest member of this group I should like to know your plans for us. Just how long do you expect to keep us here?"

He shrugged. "A week, possibly a fortnight—"

"Fortnight!"

"—depending entirely on the government in Rangoon."

"You know it's outrageous!"

He smiled faintly. "Naturally for you it is outrageous but you must surely see that you're extremely valuable to us as pawns,

78

Lady Waring. It is not every day we catch such big fish as Europeans wandering through this country."

"What do you expect to gain from this?"

He leaned comfortably against the wall of the archway. "Come now, you must not pretend such innocence. You give us life-and-death power over seven lives, and because of who you are we expect to extract much from Rangoon."

"You look Chinese to me," she said abruptly, accusingly. "Surely Wang is a Chinese name?"

His shrewd eyes rested on her with interest. "True, yes, I am Chinese from Yunnan, but the men I lead are Burmans, Shan, Kachins, Lisus, all peasants—it's their turn now at last—and if they need a Tayou, a Chinese, to show how, well—we have won our revolution, we know. You English," he said with scorn, "overestimate yourselves. You governed this country with utmost indifference for decades, destroying customs, rituals, taking oil and rice and rubies from it for yourselves, bringing in *chettyars* who robbed farmers of their land . . . You have always regarded brown skins as inferior, have you not?"

She looked at him helplessly; anger rose in her and died because in all honesty she could not deny what he said.

"There will be great changes—and you," he said dryly, "you, a member of English aristocracy, will now be one of our instruments for change."

She ignored his irony. "You want to take over this lovely country for yourselves, then?"

"You surprise me—'this lovely country'? You do not see it as backward, primitive?"

"Perhaps I did at first," she admitted. "At the moment I would prefer it to stay the way it is."

"Nothing stays the same."

"You're a fanatic, Colonel Wang."

He smiled. "I ask, will anything but fanaticism make for change? Wisdom and compromise come later."

"An intelligent fanatic," she said, nodding. "The most dangerous of all. Will we be harmed?"

"I hope not," he said pleasantly. "You must understand that you are only—as I have said—pawns on the board in a struggle for power, recognition, change. If the government in Rangoon does not pay attention, if it refuses to deal with us, I ask you, what power would be left to us if we free you in the end? Who would believe our threats after that?"

"You mean you'd *kill* us if they don't meet your terms? You've threatened Rangoon with our—our *murders?*" she said incredulously.

"But of course," he said simply, and with a polite bow he left her standing there and strode across the compound and down the hill.

Watching him go, her eyes blinking against the harsh sunlight, she thought, *How strange, how ironic, if my life should end in this country where Eric died, and the two of us be buried here . . . The others, too—so many unspent lives, all for some cause that a decade from now may be forgotten . . .* Turning she found Baharian and Miss Thorald standing several paces behind her. "You heard?" she said.

They nodded.

"The others?"

Miss Thorald shook her head and Baharian said, "They remain at the opposite side of the temple, behind the pillar, Lady Waring, they could not have heard."

She said slowly, "I think it's best they *not* know."

"With this I agree most devoutly," said Baharian. "It is not the happiest thought with which to entertain our long days and longer nights."

80

Lady Waring looked at Miss Thorald, who had reacted with neither the expected shock or fear, and she wondered at her passiveness. Such a silent woman, restful of course, thought Lady Waring, but irritating now, her incessant knitting a reminder of Madame DeFarge knitting away at the guillotine as she watched heads fall, a simile Lady Waring found appropriate if their lives were to be forfeit to a fledgling government in Rangoon. "And you, Miss Thorald?" she asked.

"Yes, I agree," she said, and turned to go back inside.

They followed but as Miss Thorald walked around the pillar an uneven paving stone tripped her and only Baharian, walking behind her, saved her from falling on the stone floor. Instead it was her knitting bag that flew across the floor, spilling out needles, wool, scissors and passport.

Mr. Gunfer leaned over and picked up the passport, glanced at it and opened it.

"That's mine, please," said Miss Thorald, quickly reaching for it.

"How very photogenic you are, Miss Thorald," he said, gazing at her passport photo. "So many of us look like ghouls in passport photos."

"Please," said Miss Thorald urgently, "please give it back, it's mine, *give it to me.*"

Lady Waring looked at her in surprise; there was nothing passive about the woman now, the urgency in her voice had silenced the others as well.

"Mr. Gunfer—" pleaded Miss Thorald.

But Mr. Gunfer's eyes had shifted, his expression turning to one of shock, and seeing this Miss Thorald's face became despairing. Lady Waring, moved by her distress, said, "Return it, Mr. Gunfer."

He said slowly and incredulously, "But this passport—with

81

her photograph attached—bears the name of Lina Thorald Lerina . . . *she's Lina Lerina.*"

Lina Lerina . . . a musical name . . . familiar, thought Lady Waring, but from long ago, before the war . . . something to do with—she stiffened in horror. She heard Mrs. Caswell give a small cry, heard Baharian whistle softly, while U Ba Sein sat against the wall watching with interest and Gen with astonishment.

It was Gen who asked, "What's wrong?"

Mr. Gunfer said fiercely, "She's a murderer, that's what. Right here—living with us. She killed her husband."

Miss Thorald said dryly, "I believe the word is murderess, not murderer."

"I don't understand," cried Gen.

Baharian was observing Miss Thorald with interest. Over his shoulder to Gen he said, "A very famous murder case, small one, in very large headlines for many months, in fact only the attack on Pearl Harbor removed it from the front pages."

"And she was convicted," gasped Mrs. Caswell.

"Yes," said Baharian. "I take it, Miss Thorald, that you seek sanctuary with a brother after being in prison since then?"

"You can take it any way you wish," said Miss Thorald, and snatching the passport out of Mr. Gunfer's hand she said in a voice thick with emotion, "That passport was mine, not yours, Mr. Gunfer, and you had no right to pry into it like that. Until this minute I was just another traveler on the steamer, now you rake up a past that I've paid for with eight years of my life, and —oh God," she cried despairingly, her voice breaking on a sob.

"Oh dear," said Mrs. Caswell.

Gen, awed by such emotion, torn by Miss Thorald's anguish, moved by loyalty, sprang to her feet and went to stand next her.

"Don't go near her," cried Mr. Gunfer, "evil is contagious—may God have mercy on her soul."

Baharian said, "God may have mercy on her soul but it would seem a little human mercy that's lacking. *Shut up, Gunfer.*"

Mrs. Caswell said again in an uncertain voice, "Oh dear."

Lady Waring stamped her cane. "Stop—all of you! Miss Thorald," she said, turning to her, "you can understand our shock. Thrown together as we are by accident I'm sure you can understand our reactions at learning one among us is a convicted murderer. An element of trust becomes very necessary among us all, and so you will also, I hope, understand why it is necessary to our well-being to ask: if you really are the Lina Lerina who killed her husband ten years ago, *who and what are you now?*"

Gen glanced up at Miss Thorald, who was gazing at Lady Waring in astonishment; her astonishment turned to anger and she said unsteadily, "That's certainly not the business of anyone in this room." Looking from face to face she added bitterly, "Let's just say I've not murdered any of *you* . . . not yet." Suddenly aware of Gen she said stiffly, "Thank you, Gen," and walked past the pillar toward the archway and the step.

U Ba Sein interrupted the silence that followed. "Excuse me, such memories amaze me, this happened ten years ago?"

Baharian nodded. "Ah yes but it was before the war, a time of great innocence, when a murder in New York City could still sell newspapers everywhere. But it is in my memory that it was not quite an ordinary trial because this man Arno Lerina was well known, he had some popularity as a crooner."

"A what?"

"A singer of sentimental love ballads, Mr. Ba Sein, in nightclubs and on radio. He had also a very pretty face, I recall, which made the murder very emotional and exciting to those who enjoy such matters."

"And she was convicted of killing him . . ."

"By both popular and jury votes, yes. I believe what preserved her from the death penalty was that it was not a premeditated murder, and that witnesses were produced who testified that this Arno Lerina had an ugly temper and the regrettable habit of hitting people—knocking them about—when angry."

Mrs. Caswell said with a shiver, "It equaled the Lizzie Borden case, you know, it was in the papers for months and months, the murder itself and then the trial—and she so beautiful!"

Baharian said dryly, "I recall a few people who felt it was her beauty that convicted her."

"Nonsense," snapped Mr. Gunfer, "she killed him, didn't she? Ran him through with a carving knife. They counted how many plunges of the knife?"

"She must surely hear everything you're saying," Gen protested. "She's not that far away, sitting on the step."

"I'm surprised you've forgotten how many plunges of the knife," said Baharian, "or perhaps in time you'll recall?"

Gunfer glared at him. "You make light of it, how dare you! For myself, how I'm ever to sleep with a murderess in the same room I don't know."

"This I am delighted to hear," said Baharian. "I've not wanted to mention it but you are a very noisy sleeper and snore hideously."

"I wonder," mused Lady Waring.

"It's quite horrid to learn who she is," said Mrs. Caswell, "but—she does seem very nice."

"You can't mean you like her!" gasped Mr. Gunfer.

"Well," began Mrs. Caswell and stopped, looked confused,

rallied and said defiantly, *"You* liked her, didn't you? Before you looked into her passport?"

"We all found her unobtrusive and very courteous," intervened Lady Waring, "but I feel distinctly uneasy about this. Pleasant as Miss Thorald seems to be, we know nothing about her temper under stress and I recall that there is both a knife"— she nodded to Gen—"and a carving tool"—here she nodded at Mr. Ba Sein—"and I feel that it would be wise to keep them under guard. I'm not accustomed to associating with people who take a life but I would imagine—" She hesitated, searching her own feelings of revulsion. "I would imagine that once having taken a life it is perhaps not so difficult, in a moment of passion—after all, she *is* a convicted murderer."

"Murderess," pointed out Baharian.

She said indignantly, "I find your attitude difficult to understand, Mr. Baharian, but since you introduced yourself as an adventurer—"

"No, it was *you* who introduced the word, Lady Waring. What I am trying to point out is that if we're to survive this— this situation—with death always a possibility, and *not* from Miss Thorald, as you well know," he said deliberately, "we can at least try to get along with one another. Nothing is going to change the fact that Miss Thorald is here with us, you have no choice about it."

U Ba Sein gave a delicate cough. "Excuse me," he said, "but certainly—surely—there is choice in *attitude,* is there not? We have been imprisoned for three days . . . Here is a woman who has already experienced eight *years* of imprisonment— which is surely a matter of interest—and for myself I have noticed that she carried in her bag one razor blade but no razor, which also interests me when I observe that her sleeves are long and remain pulled down to hide her wrists . . ."

Baharian gave him a thoughtful glance.

"Nevertheless," said Lady Waring, "this is very jarring. No one else among us has murdered anyone."

"Can you be sure?"

Her mouth dropped open in astonishment. "How dare you!"

Mr. Ba Sein smiled. "There are so many forms of murder, are there not? Small murders, small deaths . . ." His eyes looked into hers so knowledgeably that she found herself breathless for a second. Small murders . . . *I mustn't allow this,* she thought, disconcerted, and leaned her head back against the wall and closed her eyes to shut out Mr. Ba Sein's penetrating gaze. She understood what he was implying: *I'm vulnerable today,* she thought, *why am I suddenly remembering all the times I killed the eager, loving, child-confidences of Jane and Barbara by indifferent or snubbing remarks; why is this man recalling to me all the hatreds, angers and revenges I've nursed in my life?* She thought wearily, *I grow old and wounds mount but how many wounds have I given as well?* There entered into her memory a dinner party given long ago at which a guest—scientist or philosopher—had announced that people misunderstood death, they died not of too little life but of too much life, that as the skin withered and the future grew short it was the past that took on flesh, until ultimately the sheer accumulation of experience and memory became too heavy to carry.

Perhaps I've already lived too long, she thought. *Murders have been done to me and I have made very sweet revenges but Mr. Ba Sein is right, one need not wield a knife or shoot a gun to kill life, let him without sin cast the first stone.*

Miss Thorald was still sitting on the step of the temple when Gen came looking for her. "I want to understand," Gen told her. "I thought you had some wonderful secret I could learn so

I could be like you. Like a lotus. I thought you must be very wise."

Miss Thorald turned her head to her and said, "One learns a little wisdom in a prison . . . too late."

"But you have taken life, like a low Buddhist who kills for food." Struggling with this Gen said, "It's not that I haven't seen people kill—I have seen this—but that was war."

Miss Thorald nodded. "There are sometimes marriages that are like a war."

"Not love?"

"Love and hate . . . jealousy, anger, possession. I will say this, Gen, because you will be a woman too, and when Mr. Ba Sein said that I experienced eight years of prison this was not true, I was in prison long before that—all my life, really."

"What do you mean?"

She smiled. "You want me to list for you all my faults and flaws? There was vanity above all, because I was always admired for my prettiness, and so I became ambitious. Spoiled, actually, and greedy, and because of this—which I've had many years to think about—I attracted the wrong kinds of men, men so afraid they'd lose me, so wanting to prove themselves, and so jealous, that they could be cruel. And because I'd never grown up, because I'd relied only on how I looked, I had no way to deal with cruelty, I accepted it, until—until—"

"Was he cruel, then?" asked Gen.

"My lawyer pleaded self-defense at my trial," said Miss Thorald. "That was very ironic, for it would have been kinder if I'd learned self-defense years earlier. And walked away—just left . . . Be wiser than I, Gen!"

Gen thought about her words, and then, "What is it like to kill?"

"Two people die," said Miss Thorald. *"Two* lives end."

Gen nodded. "And what will you do in the village where your brother is a missionary?"

From behind them Baharian said, "Penance, obviously." Sitting down on the step between them he said, "Sorry, Miss Thorald, but can you imagine how difficult it is not to eavesdrop? I, Terence Baharian, confess to much curiosity about—" Swiftly he reached for her hand and before she could snatch it away he pushed up the long sleeve of her blouse. "I see that the wise Mr. Ba Sein was right, how many times have you tried this?"

Gen's eyes widened at the long puckered white scars running up and down and across her wrist.

Miss Thorald was silent.

He said deliberately, "What an ego trip! What self-pity to do this!"

Miss Thorald gasped. "How dare you!" she cried, leaping to her feet.

Rising to face her he said, "Your nostrils flare beautifully when you're angry but you are a coward, Miss Thorald, a coward."

"Oh you know nothing—*nothing!*" she flung at him, turned to run out into the compound, saw the guards, turned helplessly and gasped, "This awful place!" and ran inside.

Baharian, seeing Gen's startled face, said, "Well, small one?"

Gen's voice trembled. "Ma Nu would say an evil nat owns people at such times but in America I do not think they believe in nats. U Baharian, what happens to people to make them so mixed up and miserable?"

"Life happens."

"You mean kan," Gen said, nodding. "But you were cruel, weren't you?"

"The beautiful Miss Thorald wishes to hide, she wishes to

throw away the rest of her life because of her past." He shrugged. "Me, I do not like waste. It is possible she will find—what is that prim word, *redemption?*—doing missionary work with a brother—that is what Victorian novelists tell us—but it is more likely she will feel lonely and alien, and every passion in her will be killed." He added wryly, "She must be watched, that one, she has killed a husband, now she would find ways to kill the self in her, a second murder for which there would be no public trial."

It was late afternoon when Lady Waring heard a heartbroken cry from Gen, who was seated under the archway on the step. She held up a hand to still the bickering between Gunfer and Baharian, and silencing them, they heard it, too.

They rushed to the doorway, Baharian almost running into the pillar in his haste. The two soldiers playing dominoes in the shade of the guard house jumped to their feet and leveled rifles at them but only Miss Thorald noticed this. The others stared at what Gen had seen: the steamer *Khayioe* was passing under the hill, leaving a silvery wake of V's behind it as it headed downriver on its return trip to Rangoon.

Gen put both hands to her face. "I should have been with them, that's my steamer," she whispered but no one heard her and she bit her lip to keep from crying.

It was Mrs. Caswell who burst into tears. "We've been forgotten—they've abandoned us! My husband—oh, they've forgotten us!" she cried, and she turned and beat her fists against the wall of the temple, screaming the words over and over until Baharian stepped up to her, turned her around, said, "My dear lady, forgive me," and slapped her hard across the face.

8

BY EVENING a semblance of peace had been established with the lighting of a fire, the charcoal and bricks having been brought to them with their rice, and an iron kettle bestowed upon them as well. With this second meal of the day they sipped boiled water flavored with a few leaves of Gen's tea, and for dessert divided Mr. Gunfer's bars of chocolate. "But I am still hungry," complained Lady Waring. "And I will never eat rice again, never."

The steam from the kettle had contributed a healing warmth to exacerbated nerves, and following Gen's outburst and Mrs. Caswell's hysterics the bickering had died for want of fuel. Huddled around the dying fire, the flickering light throwing bizarre shadows across their faces, they looked to Gen like witches and warlocks from a book of fairy tales that she'd cherished in Maymyo before the war. Except for Miss Thorald, she amended, whose hair the firelight had turned into flame-gold. She was glad to see that U Baharian had approached Miss Thorald and was calmly asking for her favored passages in Emerson. U Ba Sein sat cross-legged with his eyes closed and Lady Waring's eyes were closed, too, as she sipped her tea—she was imagining herself back in England—while Mr. Gunfer stared sulkily into the fire and Mrs. Caswell slumped against the pillar looking pale and depleted.

Gen thought it a dreary scene; it had been a difficult day, and night was still to come, and a miasma of unspoken hostility hung over the room.

Suddenly Mrs. Caswell spoke. "I wonder," she said. Her voice faltered, rallied, she said almost angrily, "I really think— yes, there's something I want to ask . . . no, suggest."

U Ba Sein was the only one who did not look surprised. In spite of their being only seven in number Mrs. Caswell had been persistently overlooked, except for her hysterics of the afternoon, which had drawn their reluctant attention and was remembered now only with embarrassment.

"Which—ask or suggest?" said Mr. Gunfer disagreeably.

She lifted her chin and straightened her shoulders, an act that led Gen to look at her more closely, and with sympathy. With a quick glance at Mr. Gunfer she said, "I've been thinking—re-membering—something that happened to me once, and I don't see why I shouldn't speak of it, I *want* to speak of it." Her voice was defiant.

Baharian said cordially, "Please do, Mrs. Caswell."

"Thank you," she said. "I was remembering it because I feel —rather upset just now, and I admit lonely and a little fright-ened. It's something that happened to me in Africa, in fact not long ago at all."

91

"Your husband was doing archaeological work there?" asked Baharian politely.

She shook her head. "No—that is, we'd been in the Sudan, excavating in the desert, but I'd had sunstroke and was very tired, and so he made arrangements for me to go south to Northern Rhodesia for a week—on safari—because it's higher there, you see, and he thought the altitude and the change would do me good." She stopped, remembering, and with a timid smile said, "I won't bore you with how invigorating it turned out to be for me—the cool nights, the camping, the evenings around a fire, the good sleeps, the game viewing by Land Rover during the days—except to say that I learned during those five days certain things about the bush country, such as how very dangerous it was and is at night, when the bush belongs to the animals and the wildlife, not only animals but snakes as well—snakes that can kill in seconds . . .

"I loved all of it but when we reached the last lodge," she said, "I felt it had all ended because it was such a civilized place —with a bar, a swimming pool and other people. It was run by a woman who asked if I'd seen a lion and I had to say no, it was the one sight I'd missed. She insisted that I go out that night because there'd been a lion kill two miles from the lodge but I very politely thanked her and said I'd retire early. Just the same, when it had grown dark—the night falls very quickly there, and early, like a curtain dropping—she came for me and said the men were waiting in the Land Rover, eager to show me lions, so I finally shrugged and went . . .

"There were five men," she continued. "The guide, the assistant guide, the driver, another young man and most important of all the rifle bearer, for this was night in the bush. They turned on their powerful searchlight and off we went in the Land Rover, speeding down this rutted road at about fifty miles

an hour, and after driving for some time the driver shot off
through the tall grass, the grass thinned and ahead of us I could
see the carcass of a buffalo, and two lions feeding on it . . .''

When she hesitated it was Baharian who said, "Go on."

She nodded. "Of course the lions—with the searchlight on
them—immediately raced away, off to the right somewhere
through the tall grass, and it was at this point that the driver
took off after them—following them, you see—and driving at
this incredible speed over the ruts until suddenly—very
abruptly—the Land Rover hit a marshy place and came to a
crashing halt. The men jumped out to push, and I started to get
out, too, to help—being quite accustomed to pushing cars and
doing things like that," she said simply, "but this absolutely
shocked the guide. I was his charge, you see, a tourist from a
great distance—oh he was *very* firm, I had to sit while they
worked. It made me feel like a memsahib but I sat." She smiled
faintly. "And they pushed and they pushed and they pulled and
pulled but still the Land Rover was stuck.

"That's when, after considerable discussion in their own language—Nyanja, I believe it was—they came to a decision,
which was that they would walk the two miles back to camp to
get help—bring another Land Rover with chains to pull the jeep
out of the swamp—and I was to stay there and wait, with one of
the young men to keep me company.

"Of course I asked, 'and the rifle bearer, will he stay with
me?' No, the guide said, the rifle bearer would go with *them*. So
I was being told to stay in this Land Rover and wait for an hour
or so, with the lions off somewhere to the right, and to the left
of us the buffalo carcass, to which the lions would surely be
returning, and this vehicle squarely between them, with me sitting in it.

"And I was appalled," she said. "I simply knew I couldn't sit

93

there in the bush at night waiting but they looked on me as this memsahib, you see—there was that kind of distance between us . . . I heard myself say, 'No . . . no I'm going with you.' It was the firmest statement I'd ever made in my life." She paused and gave them an apologetic smile. "I am usually quite shy and timid but I couldn't even *consider* anything else. They protested but I knew I absolutely couldn't stay there and I firmly climbed out of the Land Rover and joined them . . . What I'd not realized, though, was that no one had a flashlight, there was only the searchlight, which was attached to the Land Rover, and of course that was turned off as soon as we left, plunging us into the darkest of darkness so that I took a few steps and stumbled. The guide helped me up, I walked a few more steps and fell over an anthill, and this time when the guide helped me up I said, 'We've simply got to hold hands or I'll keep stumbling and falling.' I could feel their surprise at this but I grasped the hand of the man on my left, and then the hand of the man on my right, and we formed this chain—all six of us holding hands— and resumed walking again in the darkness, and I can tell you that it was such incredible darkness at that point—in the tall grass—that if a lion had leaped out at us I'm sure the rifle bearer would never have had time to kill it. But oddly—and it *was* odd —I didn't think of this at all at the time. We walked—holding hands—and as we walked we began to talk."

Her face had become radiant in the firelight and Gen, staring at her, thought *she's turned beautiful, how did it happen?*

"We walked, and we talked," she said, "the six of us under that huge dark sky peppered with brilliant stars, and the men began asking me how I came to be in their country and if I had children, a husband . . . The guide—his name was Kulumbala, I remember—began to speak of his own family and of how he'd walked forty miles to visit his home the week before, some of it by night . . . and one by one the others chimed in with stories of their own: their village life, their children, how seldom they saw them . . .

"And the thing was," she said, "I'd stopped being a memsahib and a stranger, and we had become fellow human beings alive in the universe at the same moment. Something flowed between us, a warmth, a recognition—from holding hands and being together on this long walk at night in the bush. I wasn't frightened—it didn't occur to me to be frightened—not then—because what I felt was—oh, an incredible awareness of the moment and of the sharingness between us."

She was silent and then she said, "I've never forgotten it, I never will and what I think I'd like to ask—" She stopped, embarrassed, and then, "I think it might be lovely—could be helpful—helpful to *me* at least—if for just a minute or two we could hold hands."

No one spoke. Gen drew a deep breath and smiled at Mrs. Caswell, and then Baharian said softly, "But I think—yes—this is a most beautiful idea."

"Corny," sniffed Mr. Gunfer. "Corny as hell."

"Be quiet," Lady Waring told him, and to Mrs. Caswell, with a twisted little smile, "I don't mind."

"Would you prefer I leave?" asked Miss Thorald politely.

"Yes," said Mr. Gunfer.

"No," said Lady Waring.

"I'd like to hold hands and make a circle," Gen said eagerly, and she reached out to U Ba Sein on her left and to Miss Thorald on her right.

The circle was completed awkwardly, with a certain amount of self-consciousness, and then they all looked at each other, hands linked, until Lady Waring said abruptly, as if stung by intimacy, "I think I want to sleep now."

95

"Yes," said Mrs. Caswell, and as hands parted she added quietly, "Thank you."

But something had changed, thought Gen. She herself felt a little less lonely with these people, and for a moment Mrs. Caswell had been beautiful and would never look so plain again, Miss Thorald had been included in the circle and for that brief span of time the temple had become a temple again.

9

A CANDLE BURNED all night: Mrs. Caswell, released from her griefs and tensions, had abandoned herself to the reading of *Vampire Love* and Gen, waking from time to time, would see the glow behind the pillar before she slept again. Nevertheless when the darkness behind the wall slits turned flannel gray Gen woke up, catlike, ready and waiting for the removal of the gate, determined to be one of the two who would bring up water this morning.

As intimations of day reached them and the sky grew paler the others stirred and Mrs. Caswell, blowing out her candle, announced that she had finished reading *Vampire Love*.

"I can't tell you how restful it was," she told them. "Such an exciting book, with this wonderfully romantic hero—it quite took my mind off things. Mr. Gunfer, how did you happen to have it with you?"

He said crossly, "Found it on the steamer. Books in English being hard to come by here, I picked it up. Looks a bloodthirsty piece of trash."

"No, no, it's wonderful escapism," protested Mrs. Caswell.

"Exactly—escapism," he snarled. "Think of the worthwhile books never published or sold, books about life, death, reality, the important things, and you speak of *escapism!*"

Lady Waring said tartly, "Since the word 'escape' has an especially beautiful sound to us just now, Mr. Gunfer, it scarcely seems a moment to expound on it with such contempt. What's the book about, Mrs. Caswell?"

"A castle in the forest—haunted, Lady Waring," she said eagerly. "This innocent young girl Charmian and her brother stumble across it in a storm, there's a strange old man who warns them away, saying there are vampires—beware—but they pay no attention. But when they find this handsome young man wandering through the castle—his name is Rudolfo—at once they assume he's a ghost or, worse, the vampire, and—"

Miss Thorald said, "Could I read it next?"

"I'll put in my order, too," said Baharian.

Lady Waring interrupted him and held out her hand. "Let me see for myself, if you please." And with a scornful glance at Mr. Gunfer she plucked the book from Mrs. Caswell's lap and disappeared behind the pillar to settle down and sample *Vampire Love.*

It was curious, thought Gen, how quickly they had all marked out spaces for themselves in the temple. Instinctively and without consultation the rear of the building had become their living quarters, as if to remove them as far as possible from the hostile world outside and from the surveillance of the guards. It was here they built their fire, boiled their water and ate their rice, and here that they unfolded their blankets and slept. The area near the entrance, of equal size, was used only sparingly, but there was more than this: she noticed that each of her companions zealously guarded the spaces they'd chosen and honored those of the others, too. Mr. Gunfer had established his roots in the south corner while Miss Thorald had appropriated the opposite corner, with Lady Waring and Baharian occupying the long wall between them. Mrs. Caswell liked to sit with her back against the central pillar facing Lady Waring, and therefore this was where she slept while Gen had settled at the edge of the pillar facing U Ba Sein, who spread his blanket next to Miss Thorald along the wall. Once established it had become unspoken law that none of these spaces be violated and Gen, remembering the prison compound in Rangoon, was learning that not only missionaries had a need to make a space entirely their own, even if it measured only six feet by three.

Mrs. Caswell, folding her blanket, called over to Gen, "What's that word again for earning merit?"

"*Kutho.*"

Mrs. Caswell sighed heavily. "I so wish I had paper to write things down."

Mr. Gunfer, following Gen around the pillar, said awkwardly, "You had—I saw—a little crossword puzzle magazine in your bag."

A plea was detectable and Gen turned to look at him, at the thin vulpine face made longer by his pointed goatee, and looking into his eyes it occurred to her that he was afraid—of people, perhaps—and certainly he did not like to ask for anything. "Yes," she said.

The approach made, the preliminaries dealt with, his usual temper returned. "Then to prevent me from going quite mad with boredom, one might ask if it could be borrowed?"

"It's for children," she pointed out. "You know—what's a four-letter word for car and that sort of thing."

"Thank you but I will soon become a child myself if steps aren't taken," he said curtly. "A few more days of idleness and my brain—of which I'm quite fond—will have become too addled even to translate the word *car* into *auto*."

She fetched her puzzle book for him, reminding him to pencil in the entries lightly, so they could be erased, and hearing voices outside she hurried to the door to wait: the gate was lifted inch by inch and then carried away. *"Mayela,"* Gen called out cheerfully to the three guards, and in turn they told her they were fine and withdrew, grinning, to their hut while Gen sat down on the step and hugged her knees, anticipating her few moments of freedom at the river. Presently two of the guards reappeared with water buckets, U Ba Sein joined her and they set out for the river under guard.

It was a glorious time of day, somnolent, slow to wake, tender, peaceful, the birds chattering, singing, fluttering away at their approach. They descended among toddy palms and thorn trees, passing one mimosa tree whose fragrance followed them all the way down the hill. Across the river lay the soft green of paddies and in the distance, rising above the dawn's mist, a pagoda interrupted the flowing line of blue hills. It was an hour when the *pongyis* in the villages would be making their rounds with their black lacquer alms bowls, pausing at each house for gifts of rice or fish, and when the banks of the river at Theingyu would be lined with villagers brushing their teeth or washing their clothes, a garden of colorful longyis spread out on the banks to dry. The guards were silent, the sun had not yet risen but there was a glowing brilliance in the east.

Reaching the shore Gen walked eagerly into the water, grateful to its shock of coolness. She filled her bucket and U Ba Sein's bucket as well and carefully washed her face and hands. The two guards, relaxed, lighted cheroots and watched U Ba

100

Sein as he searched among the debris along the shore. There were no other soldiers to be seen, which was what Gen had come to learn, and this pleased her. The steamer might have gone but freedom was still possible if she acted at the right moment and if her thamma deva would return and guide her again.

When the guards called to them she walked ashore, her ragged sneakers squirting jets of water. As she handed U Ba Sein his filled bucket he said, "Just see what I found." He held out to her a small block of wood that had drifted ashore. "It's not guava wood—guava is best for carving—but with this you can be a *pabu shaya.*"

"A carver," she mused, surprised again by a rush of pleasure happening at the precise moment that an absence of soldiers was feeding her hopes of escape. *"Ceizu timbade,"* she told him, and wondered if once again he was reading her thoughts.

They began the ascent just as the sun rose to warm their backs but the bucket was heavy and the hill was steep, and Gen felt her moment of joy fading. *I am not Zawgwi,* she thought, *who can fly through the air or wave a wand to change matters, I am still Gen and still captive and perhaps even wanting to be free makes me captive.*

Baharian stood under the arch waiting to carry their buckets inside. Not far from the door Lady Waring sat reading *Vampire Love;* Gen and U Ba Sein sank down on the step to rest.

U Ba Sein said with a glance at her face, "There is no *pyobyo sinswin*—no happiness—in you this morning."

She nodded. "I miss Theingyu," she told him with a sigh. "I miss U Hamlin, too."

At his questioning glance she began, haltingly, to tell him about U Hamlin, about what had happened to her father and of how U Hamlin had helped give him a royal funeral. Opening her thoughts to U Ba Sein, speaking of these matters on the step of the temple connected her past with the present, for she had left parts of herself behind that were sorely needed, and although she was unaccustomed to speaking of important events they pressed hard on her now. But they could overflow only to U Ba Sein, who knew how the funeral pyre had honored her father in spite of his unripe death, and who knew what she meant when she spoke of her thamma deva.

"But my thamma deva has deserted me now," she ended sadly.

They had been speaking in Burmese but now she slipped into English and U Ba Sein joined her. "Deserted you?" he said, startled. "How can you know this, how can you be sure?"

"Because I'm here," she said listlessly.

He smiled. "Yes you are here," he agreed. "Because you do not like being here you think your thamma deva has abandoned you?"

She nodded. "And there are fears, U Ba Sein, I no longer belong in Theingyu, where people are happy, and I fear I will never belong in America where I'm to go, and this frightens me."

"That is to be expected," U Ba Sein said, nodding sagely.

"Why?" she pleaded. "I don't know who I'll be, I don't know who I am. Even now!"

He said firmly, "You will be—still—a star visitor."

"A what?"

He smiled, his plump cheeks folding into creases. "A visitor from the stars."

Hugging her knees she said, *"Me?"*

"Oh yes. It's why you will always be a little lonely. It will be hard for you to belong, Zen, for how can it be otherwise when you come here as a visitor from a faraway star?"

"A visitor," she repeated, groping with this thought. "You mean I do matter—I matter somewhere, U Ba Sein?"

"Very much, yes."

"But—a star visitor from where?"

"It has many names, Zen Perris, but in the English language it would be called Octurus."

"Octurus," she said, pleased. "And I come from there? Where is it, can I see it in the night sky?"

He shook his head. "It's a master star thirty-three light-years from the sun, a place far more evolved than earth, but when you end this life—which will be an important life for you—you will return there."

"So I do have a place," she whispered. "I do have a home."

"You do have a home," he said, and they sat quietly and in peace together until Gen was called inside by Baharian.

Lady Waring, seated not far from the doorway with her book, called accusingly, "I heard what you told her, Mr. Ba Sein."

He turned. "Did you, Lady Waring?"

"You're a scoundrel but I like what you did."

"And what did I do, Lady Waring?" he said, amused.

"Gave the child confidence . . . So she goes to America, does she! It's no wonder that she's frightened when this country is all she's known." Lady Waring nodded. "You handled that very well, Mr. Ba Sein. Very imaginatively, too."

He said meekly, "Thank you so much, Lady Waring."

She said dryly, mockingly, "And I, too, will I go to this star Octurus when my life ends?"

"No, Lady Waring," he said, and excusing himself he walked past her into the temple.

In the afternoon, much to their astonishment, soldiers began bringing up the hill sections of high wooden fence from the village below. They brought them on their backs, and marched away to bring more, while three soldiers remained behind to insert posts into the ground at intervals.

As they crowded the doorway, watching, their guard wandered over and broke into lively chatter that Mr. Ba Sein translated for them. "He says now we can breathe fresh air and walk, for they make us a second *khan*—a second room."

"But we won't be able to see the river," cried Gen. "Or the sunsets—it's cruel!"

"Let me know when they've finished," said Lady Waring, "I'm returning to *Vampire Love.* You were quite right, Mrs. Caswell—"

"Oh please call me Helen."

"Quite right about the book, Helen, it's very engrossing and it certainly takes one's mind off things."

When the fence was finished they had lost their sunsets but gained a compound; a gate had been installed at the far end, and the guard hut moved back to a position just six feet in front of it to conceal and guard this single exit. The arrangement apparently held dividends for Colonel Wang as well because two soldiers were relieved from guard duty for the afternoon, leaving only one behind, which was how Gen made her first contact with the outside world.

She had walked into the compound to hunt for grasshoppers —for herself if no one else cared to eat them—and to hunt them before they disappeared from the several patches of high grass in the enclosure. She crept through and around the small jungles of grass, catching them with cupped hands and dropping them into her empty bucket, using her hat as a lid to keep them inside. She had caught six when she became aware of the guard making persistent hissing sounds at her. She crossed the compound to the hut where he sat on a bench under its one window, rifle in his lap.

"You make noises like a *mwei,*" she told him. *"Ba loujinoale—* what do you want?"

Without reply he turned and pointed behind him, which is when she saw the figure hiding in the shadows between hut and gate. She started to say, "Who—" and then she recognized him. "Ba Tu?" she said incredulously. "Ba Tu, you've found me?"

"You're okay," he said in relief as she went to him. "Ma Nu was afraid for you, but don't talk so loud, Zen, and stay in the shadow!"

"You've seen Ma Nu? Have you also seen the man I was with on the hill? Is he safe? It's important, Ba Tu, have you seen U Hamlin?"

"He wasn't captured with you?"

Gen's heart sank; he had not been seen, then, but had vanished like mist at dawn; she could only shake her head, wordless.

"I've seen nothing of him, Zen, but when I went back to Theingyu to tell my mother where you were, Ma Nu said there was news of many soldiers in the area where I found you and the stranger. She sent me back to warn you but too late!"

She nodded. "I was captured only hours after seeing you, Ba Tu, but how did you find me?"

He grinned. "Sometimes it is good to be a *damya.* This chap on guard here is a friend, he was a dacoit once, too, his name is Ko Thein but now he's chosen to be a soldier for a while. We met in the village down the hill and when he told me there were Europeans in the temple I asked if there was a girl here who speaks Burmese and he said yes, a thin one with a funny hat." He laughed. "I said yes, that's Zen, but I had to wait until

105

he was sent to guard you again. I had to see you and make sure you're okay, Zen, but I can't stay long."

She said urgently, "Ba Tu, I have to get out of here—we all have to get out, I grow worried, I must get to Rangoon!"

Ba Tu nodded. "I'll see what I can do. You know Ma Nu will never let me in the house again if I don't help you!"

"What do you think you can do?"

He wrinkled his brow in thought. "There are soldiers everywhere, there would be no way to get you away by land. It would have to be by boat, but—"

"I have money, Ba Tu. The gold watch and money."

"Ah! That will help." His face brightened. "Give me some kyat, I'll put it to good use and see what can be done. How many are with you in the temple?"

"Six."

He said thoughtfully, "For so many people it would need three boats, I think, but how to get you out of here and down the hill to boats I don't know. Six miles to the south—maybe only five—there are no soldiers. If we can find boats to get you downriver—"

"All of us?"

"Okay—all of you," he promised. "Trust me, Zen, you know you are like a *thami* to Ma Nu."

"Give her a hug for me, Ba Tu."

"You can give *me* one!"

She flashed a smile at him. "Okay—there! Now I'll get the money for you. Wait!"

"Be quick!"

She sped back into the temple, and because Mr. Gunfer was in the middle of another argument with Lady Waring and with Baharian, she was able to extract from her bag three hundred of her eight hundred kyat. Returning to Ba Tu she slipped the bills into his hand, and having gained time to think she told him, "Every morning two of us go under guard to the river for water, Ba Tu. There's a big rock down there next to a toddy palm —you could hide a message under it and I'd find it when it's my turn to get water."

He nodded. "I can do that but don't expect one too soon." With a wave to Ko Thein he vanished through the half-opened gate, leaving Gen excited and pleased.

What a surprising day, she thought: she had learned that she was a star visitor and she had received fresh hope of escape from Ba Tu . . . Returning to the bucket that she'd abandoned in the grass she squatted down beside it; a second later she dropped to the earth and sat hugging her knees while she considered what to tell the others in the temple. The sun beat down on her head and she missed her hat but of course it was holding the grasshoppers captive, she could hear them leaping against the sides of the bucket in their attempts to be free.

She thought, *Fishermen don't part lightly with their boats, even for a day. Ba Tu may find one boat quickly but two boats will need more time and more money, and he said three . . . is it wise to tell the others about Ba Tu today?*

The rhythmic struggles of the grasshoppers distracted her. She thought of the delicacy of their pale green wings and imagined how they must be yearning for the cool tall grass and its shade; they would soon enough tire from their efforts.

It will surely be kinder to say nothing of Ba Tu's visit yet, she decided, and in her mind she counted over her reasons: there were first of all the boats to find, as well as a way to move seven people down to the river, but the most important reason of all was that her temple companions occupied themselves all day by talking in loud voices, and they might be heard speaking of this matter as they digested her news. She decided that it would be too much food for them; as Ma Nu said, A wise man knows too much food is poison. This would be her secret, they all had secrets and this would be hers.

She stood up and carried the bucket across the compound to the nearest fence and stood below it. Reaching under the hat into the bucket she gently removed one of the grasshoppers, held it up, whispered, "Jump high!" and tossed it over the fence. Six times she did this, absorbing into herself their joy at being free, and then she picked up the empty bucket and went back into the temple.

10

THAT EVENING, crouched around the coals of their cooking fire, Lady Waring closed the book *Vampire Love* and nodded. "Very satisfying," she said, and smiled pleasantly at Mr. Gunfer. "We certainly thank you for rescuing it from the boat. Incidentally, how long have you been a travel writer, Mr. Gunfer?"

He looked startled by this unexpected amiability. "Not long."

"How long?" she pressed him.

"I told you, not long. Actually I consider Burma a real feather in my cap, I plan a book—or did," he added. "I've had two or three articles published in travel magazines but I'm counting on this to establish me."

"Interesting," she murmured. "Whereabouts on the steamer did you find the book?"

He shrugged. "Tucked behind the bunk in the cabin."

"That, too, I find interesting," she continued amiably, "especially since I note that the copyright date of the book is 1949 and we are only a few days into the first month of 1950—a very recent book," she said deliberately, "and I understand that we're the first non-Burmese people allowed to travel on the river since insurgency broke out. One wonders who could have hidden the book there."

Mr. Gunfer looked startled. "Very mysterious, yes, now that you mention it."

"What's the matter?" asked Gen, aware of an undercurrent beneath Lady Waring's pleasantness, and of a growing tension.

"Not quite so mysterious as one might think," said Lady Waring, her voice sharpening. "I don't believe you just happened to find this book in your cabin, Mr. Gunfer, I think you must have brought it with you from America, isn't that so?"

"Nonsense," said Mr. Gunfer, and Gen thought that even his goatee quivered with indignation.

"I also think," said Lady Waring calmly, "that you wrote the book, Mr. Gunfer . . . I think you're Cynthia Gore."

"I *beg* your pardon!" gasped Mr. Gunfer.

Holding up the book she said, "I dare you to deny it."

He gaped at her, closed his mouth with a snap and said, "This is preposterous, what's worse insulting."

"Mr. *Gunfer?*" breathed Helen Caswell.

Baharian said, "What makes you think—?"

"A real author?" said Gen eagerly.

"Stop—stop!" cried Mr. Gunfer. "This is outrageous!"

"You see, I began to notice all the phrases in the book identical to ones that you use in conversation," she told him. "In fact I heard your voice in so many places, especially Rudopho's. No, I'll amend that," she said, "it didn't begin to haunt me until page twenty-seven and then—"

110

"Ridiculous," said Gunfer.

"—and then of course," she continued, "I also found it mystifying as to how such a recent paperback book in English had reached Burma, halfway around the world from New York. It's true that a certain number of foreign experts are arriving in this country to help in its recovery from the war, and one of them could have brought it along, but I can't believe that any of them would have chosen to travel upcountry on a steamer that takes ten days to reach Mandalay. Then, too, I was told with great authority in Rangoon that no Europeans had been allowed on the river until now, it was simply not considered safe. I was told this over and over again, and certainly the consulates, the ministries and the shipping line wouldn't all of them lie about it. Come, come, Mr. Gunfer, admit that you're the author of—" Consulting the book's jacket she said, *"The Secret of the Labyrinth, Mrs. Carlisle's Folly, Blood on the Moon,* and *Vampire Love."*

To their utter astonishment Mr. Gunfer burst into tears.

"Stop, I can't bear it—don't," he sobbed, and buried his head in his hands. "Don't—it's too—too *humiliating,* you can't understand how humiliating."

"What is?" asked Mrs. Caswell.

"To be found out?" asked Miss Thorald.

"No no," he cried. "To be accused of writing anything so—so superficial and inane."

"Now you're insulting me," said Lady Waring coldly. "Not to mention Helen—Mrs. Caswell. You don't deny you're their author?"

"No," he said miserably. "No, I wrote them."

"And how did *that* happen?" said Baharian, looking amused.

Gunfer's face was wet with tears; U Ba Sein reached into his longyi and politely handed him a shred of cloth with which to dry his eyes.

"It happened because—oh I wrote such a splendid book," Gunfer said, gulping down a sob. "Such an important book . . . maybe you've heard of it, *The Eye of God?*" When no one responded he said bitterly, "No, of course not, nobody heard of it. It was a novel about—about the darkness of man's soul," he said, his voice turning eloquent. "About trial, doubt, illusions and delusions, the destruction of hope, the renascence of spirit . . . it was a book I poured myself into—it was my *life's work,* and the reviewers—" A sob escaped him. "The reviewers—the two who reviewed it—called it pretentious and boring." He added savagely, "And it sold only nine hundred and twenty-three copies."

"Doesn't sound a very cheerful book," commented Baharian.

"Spare me," said Gunfer acidly. "Is *life* cheerful? My book plumbed its depths, it *spoke.*"

"To nine hundred and twenty-three people, yes," said Baharian.

"And five years devoted to writing it!" cried Mr. Gunfer with passion. "Five years of hope and dedication and living on day-old bread and canned beans, working day and night and when it was over I had *nothing.*" He said angrily, "That's when I sat down and angrily wrote *The Secret of the Labyrinth* in four weeks —*four weeks!*" he cried in an anguished voice. "And it was published and sold thirty-five thousand copies."

Mrs. Caswell nodded. "I read that one, too, it was really exciting and quite fun."

"Fun!" shuddered Gunfer. "Pure escapism!"

"Yes, from darkening souls and destruction of hope," said Baharian dryly.

"You make fun of me!" shouted Gunfer. "You enjoy humiliating me!"

To Gen's surprise Mrs. Caswell lifted her voice and shouted

back at him. "Don't you dare speak of *Vampire Love* that way, how dare you! Reading it I forgot to worry about Harry's blood pressure and how his blood pressure must be *skyrocketing* from worry about me, and reading it I forgot I'm hungry and I forgot I'm tired and forgot I can't walk away from this temple and go *home.* I thought you an awful man before and I think you're awful now. Worse, you're selfish through and through." And she, too, burst into tears.

This time it was Baharian who patiently supplied the handkerchief for her to wipe away tears.

"Now see what you've done," said Lady Waring.

"See what *you've* done," Gunfer said waspishly. "Humiliation after humiliation."

U Ba Sein said, "Excuse me . . . you have been much wounded, one sees this, Mr. Gunfer, but is it that you do not wish to give people pleasure?"

He was ignored, for Gunfer was still confronting Lady Waring. "I'll never forgive you for this," he said in a venomous low voice. *"Never.* Look at you—rich, aristocratic, moving only in the best circles, thoroughly spoiled, you know nothing about compromise or prostituting yourself. You're insulated against hurts, against reality—"

She said scornfully, "You think in stereotypes, you know nothing of my life."

"I happen to be a socialist," he said warningly, "so I can guess very *accurately* how you live. No humiliations for you!"

Miss Thorald said wistfully, "He does have a point there, you know. You must have had a very romantic and glamorous life, Lady Waring, being English and a titled lady and rich."

"Really?" said Lady Waring dryly. "Then to puncture one of your misconceptions I'm not English at all, I was born one of the three Bartlett sisters of Boston, Massachusetts, and the least beautiful of us, too, I might add. Rich yes, but American, and the three of us groomed for marriages. *Important* marriages."

"You're American, too?" cried Gen.

Gunfer glared at her suspiciously. "Hard to believe."

"Is it? For fifty years I've been English, ever since I met Ambrose aboard ship on my first trip abroad, when I was eighteen and he was thirty-eight, but for eighteen years I was American, and born one."

"He was twenty years older?" Gen said doubtfully, accomplishing sums in her head. "Was he very handsome?"

"No, but he was kind," said Lady Waring. "Or seemed so to me, for I'd not known much kindness. I thought him a god, I thought—I thought too much."

"Too much why?" asked Mrs. Caswell.

"Because he was habitually and compulsively unfaithful." Turning to Mr. Gunfer she said, "You think I've never experienced humiliation? This man I married could no more look at a woman than begin an affair with her. It seemed that other women were moved by his kindness, too," she added dryly.

Shocked, Mrs. Caswell said, "Did you know that before you married?"

"Of course not," she said scornfully, "I was swept off my feet and we married two months after meeting. Nine months later Jane was born, and ten months after that came Barbara. It was two years before I lifted my head from a domestic tyranny of nannies, prams and babies to discover that the great romance I thought I occupied was only an arrangement, a sham."

With a cold glance at Mr. Gunfer she said, "You speak of humiliation, Mr. Gunfer . . . yours is private and self-inflicted, mine was very public. I was a convenience to a man who had decided to marry late and start a family to gain an heir. Heaven only knows how many affairs there'd been during the two years I was involved in the nursery."

"Oh how sad," said Mrs. Caswell.

"It chilled me," Lady Waring said. "I felt of no value at all; worse, it killed something in me."

She was silent, looking back, and they were silent, too, watching the changes of expression in her face and in her eyes.

"After that," she said, "Ambrose and I saw very little of each other. I can't say that Ambrose wasn't kind—he was, whenever we met—but once I knew about his incessant and very public infidelities—and he knew I knew—I felt nothing except betrayal."

"You stayed married," pointed out Baharian.

She nodded. "I had two daughters but most of all I had pride. And frankly," she admitted, "nowhere to go if I left, and so for years I played my part, doing all the proper things and being Lady Waring." To Miss Thorald she said, "Romantic? Exciting? No."

"Oh dear," said Mrs. Caswell with feeling.

"But didn't anything nice ever happen?" pleaded Gen. "Something happy?"

Lady Waring was silent, her eyes turned inward as she gazed into her past, and after a moment she said with a small and secret smile, "Once . . . yes, once something happened."

They waited.

"And since it scarcely matters now, perhaps—yes, I can speak of it. How strange," she said, looking into their faces one by one, "how strange to speak of it here. Now. To strangers."

"Oh please," Gen said, "I want to hear that something nice happened to you."

Lady Waring's face softened. "Thank you, my dear." She hesitated, and then, "It began because I thought—because I

115

wanted—to find a refuge from all the falseness and the pretending and the demands. An odd desire but I was nearing forty and there never seemed time to think. And so I went looking—which occupied me for several months—and found—oh, the simplest cottage in Cornwall, near the sea. A garden. A low stone wall. Five rooms. And I would go there . . .

"It happened in 1921—after another war," she said softly. "In the spring, when there were lilacs in the garden, and at a time when the only changes in my life were the changing of the seasons. There was an accident," she said. "An accident on the narrow winding road in front of my cottage."

Her voice broke, and Mr. Gunfer removed his glance from the floor and gave her a sharp glance.

"My daughters were at school in France," she went on, "and my husband in London. He had never been curious or interested in seeing my cottage, which is how things were at that time. And I was alone, blessedly alone, without even a maid or a woman from the village. A car went berserk, slammed through the wall, narrowly missing the lilac tree, and turned over when it hit the old stone well-sweep in the center of the garden."

She said dryly, "The man who was in the car had traveled all the way from Switzerland, it seemed, to plow up my garden and ruin the old well-sweep that had been there for a century."

And to change my life, she might have added.

Her voice and her eyes had grown tender, and when she began again Gen understood that she was no longer speaking to them or even aware of them, but was remembering and re-creating something important.

"I called the doctor—it was Doctor Stiner then," she said, "and the man was carried into my cottage and upstairs to the spare room where it was discovered that—miraculously—he'd suffered only concussion and a broken arm, but he was not to be moved yet, which I thought a great annoyance at the time." She smiled faintly at this. "So he slept in my spare bedroom, his face empty of expression, completely dead to me, his head a skull with thinning gray hair, his nose a shade too long between high cheekbones. He was simply *there* . . .

"One might say," she added idly, "like the furniture.

"On the second day he woke," she said, her voice quickening, "and he wasn't the same person at all—I'd forgotten how emptied a person can look when asleep . . ." She paused, remembering how those bright, interested eyes had rested on her when she'd brought him breakfast on a tray and later, coming into the kitchen from pruning her roses, how she'd found him waiting for her at the door. *You should be in bed,* she told him and he'd said, *I don't know your name . . . mine is Matthew von Damm, and yours?*

"He wanted his books," she continued, "and I brought him the heavy duffle bag that had been stowed away in the hall cupboard, and for two days I went about my small chores coming on him in strange places. He loved to talk. I remember him holding up one of his books and saying in that accented voice of his, 'Do you know Aeschylus?' I didn't know what or who he meant—and then he recited to me those words of Aeschylus written over a thousand years ago—" She closed her eyes to speak them: " 'God, whose law it is that he who learns must suffer . . . And even in our sleep pain that cannot forget falls drop by drop upon the heart and in our despair—against our will—comes wisdom to us by the awful grace of God.' " Opening her eyes she said simply, "Because of this—because of the way he spoke those lines—I knew, suddenly, a great deal about him."

At first she'd paid him little attention but gradually, unaware,

117

she'd begun to listen closely. He was a mining engineer and he seemed to have traveled everywhere—to the Sahara, to South Africa, Australia, Persia—and read widely as well, so that she began to understand what a small life she had lived, and how uneducated she was. He was humorous, too, and she was unaccustomed to humor in a man, and always she was aware of his presence and that imperceptibly the atmosphere of her cottage was changing. At first she resented this, because this was her sanctuary, her refuge.

"I would be working in the kitchen," she said, "and suddenly I'd sense he was behind me in the doorway, watching. One noontime when I was basting a chicken I glanced up and found him staring at me with great intentness, and for a long moment we looked at each other and then he turned and stamped away as if he was angry with me.

"He'd begun to have dinner with me at the little table overlooking the garden, and that evening—the doctor had told him he could leave the next day—we were very quiet. I cut his portion of chicken for him because his arm was still in a cast . . . I remember there was a small fire in the fireplace and a thick fog outside, shutting out the world, and when we'd finished dining he stood up and I went around the table to gather up his empty plates."

Her eyes closed, remembering. "As I reached over to grasp a platter my arm touched his, and it was like—like a charge of electricity between us. He said in a startled voice, 'Sara?' and I found myself incapable of moving away and I knew—" Her voice faltered. "I knew what was about to happen and I told myself it was madness, we were both mad."

She opened her eyes and said almost harshly, "It was spring and the lilacs were in bloom and the sun was warm and the fruit trees were blooming and the fragrances were summer fragrances—of fresh-cut grass, warm earth, honeysuckle—and I was nearly forty and knew nothing of love or even of tenderness so that nothing—*nothing,*" she said fiercely, "had prepared me for this sudden late awakening, this rush of passion . . ." She stopped and then, softly, "We asked nothing of each other, we simply accepted and lived it, savoring each other, enjoying, and no one knew, and four weeks later when he left—"

"Oh no," cried Gen in a heartbroken voice.

"Yes, left," Lady Waring said softly, smiling at her. "And I, too, was heartbroken for a while, Gen, and yet—it was enough, you see. I didn't understand it then but I'd been given something perfect and without flaw, and this isn't given to everyone. It was something beyond any reality we usually live in, and its price was its brevity, because it could never have been sustained. It took me a long time to see this—that it was a gift, a miracle."

There was silence, all of them watching her face, and then Miss Thorald said, "But did you never see him again, never even hear from him?"

Lady Waring hesitated, and then, "Not really, no."

Seeing that soft and secret smile, hearing the subtle irony in her voice, Gen arrived suddenly at interesting conclusions of her own. In Theingyu nothing was private, a great deal of information was exchanged each morning at the village well, and doing sums in her head Gen not only guessed but *knew,* and dared speak. "Eric happened," she said.

"Who's Eric?" asked Mr. Gunfer, finding himself diverted against his will.

"Her son," Gen said eagerly. "Her son who was killed here in Burma in 1944, during the war. She said he was twenty-two but he'd be twenty-eight now, just exactly forty years younger than Lady Waring."

"Impertinent child," said Lady Waring, but not without affection.

"Is that true?" asked Miss Thorald. "You bore Matthew's son?"

"Did your husband ever know?" asked Baharian.

Lady Waring laughed. "Yes, I think he guessed—I'm sure he did—but he finally had his son . . . and I," she said softly, "had Eric. For twenty-two years." And to her astonishment she heard herself say, "And for this I can be deeply grateful—that I knew him for twenty-two years." And with a feeling of awe she realized that what she'd heard herself say was true: there had been Eric for twenty-two years and she could be grateful.

There was a long silence and then Mr. Ba Sein said in his mild voice, "How very strange that this man came from so far away—as you have said—to crash into your garden wall one day so that you could find each other and produce not only joy but a son."

Lady Waring smiled. "Yes, as if a star crossed somewhere, rearranging and arranging life so that I would have something of my own after all."

"Stars," murmured Gen. *"Do* they cross, U Ba Sein, to make kan?"

"What's kan?" asked Miss Thorald.

"Fate," Gen told her.

Mr. Gunfer said, "Stars certainly didn't do any crossing when we ended up captives in this wretched temple!"

U Ba Sein said with a chuckle, "Can you be sure of that, Mr. Gunfer?"

Lady Waring eyed him warily. "You're a strange man, Mr. Ba Sein."

"The fire is dying," pointed out Baharian.

"Yes, it's nearly midnight," said Miss Thorald, "and if I'm to

120

read *Vampire Love* next, does anyone mind if I burn a candle and begin it now?"

"Ask Mr. Gunfer," said Lady Waring, turning to look at him with a faint smile.

Mr. Gunfer was struggling with conflicting emotions. He said testily, "If you must, go ahead." Finding them all staring at him he glanced at Lady Waring, turned away and mumbled, "I daresay an apology is in order . . . Very well," he said, "I apologize." And with this he wrapped his blanket around him and lay down.

Gen smiled across the dying fire at U Ba Sein, and then at Lady Waring, and reached for her own blanket.

"Nevertheless," said Baharian thoughtfully, "one must consider whether meetings like Lady Waring's happen by accident or by design, and whether, perhaps, such a meeting was waiting for her all the time. An interesting philosophical thought, is it not? For if one insists that events take place only at random and by chance, then you have here a most interesting situation: a traveler from a distant country choosing England to visit at a certain time, strictly by chance, and turning by chance down a certain road in a certain Cornwall village, and to this one must add a defective brake or steering apparatus that snaps at the proper moment to send him crashing into a garden at the exact moment that Lady Waring, whose natural habitat is London, is staying in that cottage, and," he added humorously, "not even out shopping for bread or cheese. Then one must also consider their obvious compatibility and the magic between them—" He shrugged. "Yes, one must ask if the events that change lives are chance, or fate." With a nod he rose to his feet. "Now you must excuse me, for one of the privileges of there being no gate at the doorway now is the luxury of visiting the latrine at midnight. I bid you goodnight," he said with a bow, and went out.

Gen wrapped her blanket close and lay down, satisfied; these people were not made of stone after all, they carried treasures and wounds inside of them and truly they were even like herself.

11

IT WAS BY HAPPENSTANCE if such existed, given Baharian's speculations of the night before, that they all became involved in puppet-making the next day. Until then Gen's conferences with U Ba Sein had taken place on the temple step, or in the farthest corner of the temple quite removed from the others; it had been noted that Gen had spent a number of hours drawing squares in Mr. Ba Sein's notebook, inside of which, under his tutelage, she had blocked out the planes of a head, learning how to plan it in three dimensions. It had also been noted that she had a habit of pursing her lips and blowing through them when she concentrated and it was assumed that she was learning how to be a *pabu shaya* and how to carve a head under Mr. Ba Sein's guidance from the square of wood that he'd found on the shore.

Presently, however, it was discovered to be impossible to

carve the block of wood without a metal clamp to hold it still, and following this Gen began whittling the block with her knife, which was dull, and in underestimating the length of the nose she inadvertently cut it off. Her disappointment was profound, and her cry of indignation so loud that it captured attention. Miss Thorald and Baharian had been talking in the corner and looked up, startled. Lady Waring had begun reading Gen's teenage magazine a second time, carefully rereading each story, article and advertisement in order to calm her growing impatience, and Mrs. Caswell, after her first lesson in Burmese from Gen, had closed her eyes to whisper over and over, *"Ti, hni, thoun, lei . . ."* She opened them now.

There were tears in Gen's eyes: this mattered, she had been feeling again that strange sense of happiness that implied a very different and unexpected genevieve inside of her, a Gen waiting to surprise her with all kinds of delights. She had looked forward to carefully following the grain of wood with her tool and slowly changing wood into personality, she had wanted to bring a puppet to life, she had wanted to *create.*

U Ba Sein only shrugged. "Puppetmasters must be resourceful," he said. "We are denied wood, we are denied pâpier-maché, there is still cloth."

"Cloth!" cried Gen in disappointment.

"We can make heads of cloth, stuff them with grass and mount them on sticks to make rod puppets. From this comes learning, too."

"Like Punch and Judy!" exclaimed Mrs. Caswell. "Oh but then you must give a show for us!"

The thought of actually creating a show somewhat assuaged Gen's disappointment at not immediately becoming a *pabu shaya.* For Lady Waring the diversion was a welcome relief from dwelling on the fact that this was their fifth day of captivity and there were no signs as yet of response or rescue from Rangoon. "What puppets will you make?" she asked. "What stories do you know?"

Gen turned to U Ba Sein. "There are the *yokthe pwe* stories, U Ba Sein, you must know them all. Could we do one of those?"

He smiled. "Abbreviated, of course." To the others he explained, "Traditionally they continue all night and sometimes for days."

"We have Zawgwi and there has to be—oh, there must be!— a prince and a princess, and if there's enough cloth there could be a balu."

"I feel that I should contribute the cloth for that one," said Lady Waring dryly.

"At least three puppets to create, then."

"And more if there's enough cloth," finished Gen.

By noontime Lady Waring had divested herself of her petticoat and Miss Thorald was unraveling her knitting to contribute strands of wool for tying the puppets to the rods. Mr. Gunfer, with nothing else to do, had actually volunteered to strip the compound of its grass, while Gen and Mr. Ba Sein took turns with Miss Thorald's scissors in cutting up Lady Waring's petticoat and eventually Baharian's undershirt, followed in late afternoon by Mr. Gunfer's undershirt and then Mrs. Caswell's petticoat. Added materials would have to wait until morning, when Gen and Mr. Gunfer would take a turn at bringing up water and could gather stalks of bamboo for the rods, and as much grass as the guards would allow them time to collect.

In the meantime there was Lady Waring's cane on which to mount their single nearly completed marionette head. It was featureless as yet, which precipitated a spirited argument as to whether it should be the princess, with some of Miss Thorald's dark wool attached as hair with their one safety pin, or whether

125

the safety pin should be saved to make a turban for the prince
with snippets of blue silk from Mr. Gunfer's shirt. When this
was interrupted by the arrival of their evening rice there was
surprise at how quickly the day had passed, at how few argu-
ments had erupted, at how vivacious Miss Thorald had been
and how compliant Mr. Gunfer had proven to be.

As they ate their rice from the common kettle, no longer
appalled at dipping into it with their fingers, Lady Waring found
herself observing Miss Thorald, noting the radiance that
lingered on her face, and she wondered.

Curiosity won. "Miss Thorald," she said.

Miss Thorald glanced up. "Yes, Lady Waring?"

"I find myself very curious about your plans," she said, impal-
ing her with a stern glance. "If we get out of this situation intact
I find it more and more difficult to picture you living on Christian charity with a missionary brother. Do you truly *want* to join
your missionary brother?"

Miss Thorald said quickly, "Of course."

"Oh you said that much too fast," Mrs. Caswell told her.
"That was *very* automatic, I think Lady Waring means do you
really?"

Miss Thorald flushed.

"Say it," demanded Lady Waring.

"Say what, that there's nowhere else for me to go?" she asked
angrily. "This is 1950, Lady Waring, nearly ten years after my
trial, and yet all of you recognized and remembered my name,
you knew it at once."

"Change your name."

"I tried," said Miss Thorald. "I tried that when I came out of
prison, I used another name, not legally but to hide behind. I
stayed in a rooming house where the landlady kept staring at
me and saying she was sure she'd seen me somewhere, so I

moved before she could remember where . . . Then I applied for a job and had to give my legal name for Social Security, and —" She shivered. "That was terrible. The sudden coolness, the politeness, nothing available after all, they said, and clerks coming to stare at me because word had gotten around that Arno Lerina's murderess was applying for work. That's when I accepted my brother's offer—his *kind* offer," she added firmly, "because where he has his school and mission there'll be no other Americans or Europeans to identify me."

"A pity that you're not one to brazen things out," Lady Waring told her. "You need anger, haven't you any anger in you, any defiance?"

"At what? At whom? I killed my husband, Lady Waring, and that was anger—cold, blazing, furious anger, an emotion I can't afford."

Mrs. Caswell said, "Would he have killed you if you hadn't killed him first?"

She shrugged. "I didn't wait to find out, did I?"

"Oh my dear," said Mrs. Caswell, "it's over and it's past, Lady Waring is right about that. To hide yourself in a small village in a foreign country—and forgive me but I *cannot* see you as a missionary's aide."

Tight-lipped, Miss Thorald said, "I have no choice."

"Here in Burma," said Gen, wanting to be helpful, "when anyone does something they're sorry about they give money to the *pongyi* or they build a pagoda to gain merit."

"More pagodas we do not need," Baharian said dryly. "I have a proposition to make to you, Miss Thorald."

"Yes?"

"I can be very charming, of course, but I am not attractive physically—oh, this I know," he said with a wave of a hand. "I am scarcely a romantic object—this I say frankly and plainly—

127

but me, I have a sense of adventure, of curiosity—and it would be of much interest how we might deal together, Miss Thorald. I could offer you a new name, a new beginning. Naturally love would not be expected, one might call it an arrangement of convenience or of inconvenience."

Miss Thorald stared at him in astonishment. *"Marriage?"*

"This shocks you?" he inquired politely.

She said, "I don't understand."

They were all of them silent, looking from Baharian to Miss Thorald, Gen with eagerness.

He said gently, "I offer you a *life.*"

"But—I have nothing to give to life," she stammered. "I died a long time ago."

"Very true, and so you have told me privately," he said with a twinkle in his eye. "But not irrevocably, one may hope."

She laughed. "How stubborn you are."

"I might add that you have appeared remarkably alive to-day," he pointed out. "We Armenians understand suffering. Like the Jews we have been persecuted and massacred but to cherish suffering—deliver me!" he said with a shudder, and turned to Lady Waring. "Of course you were most suspicious of me on our first day here, and it is true, I am a man to be suspected and I say to you now—and to Miss Thorald, too—that I am not what you think I am." He flung out his arms dramatically. "I am very modest, a mere salesman of used cars in San Francisco. On the other hand, when I bought my garage it was a shack, a hovel, and now it is a fine and bustling business. And I have also a garden.

"Because," he said ruefully, "I have a passion to watch things grow. I cannot offer much—a used car business—myself, a man of large proportions—and a garden that grows."

She was staring at him, bewildered. "Are you mad?"

128

"Oh quite," he said. "I told you, a mere proposition, a choice."

"Just because I'm—because I'm pretty?"

"Not at all," he responded. "Because of the life teeming inside of you . . . also because I like you and because from suffering I see you growing like a garden." He shrugged. "Maybe also because you read Lao-tse . . . and maybe also because of what you are now, which is too much to waste on martyrdom."

She cried indignantly, "Martyrdom!"

"You do not see it? Of course martyrdom!"

"Impossible," she said firmly. "I like you but it's absolutely impossible."

"Because *I* am not pretty?"

"Oh you don't understand," she flung at him, "I'd bring ruin to anyone!"

"That would be for me to decide," he said gently. "Can you entertain the possibility that it would be kinder—even happier —than doing penance in a village up near the border of this country?"

"I thought you were here to hunt for someone's gold."

He shrugged. "That is what brought me here—or so I *thought,*" he said with a smile at U Ba Sein.

"You couldn't be sure I'd not kill you, too," she said bitterly.

Baharian grinned. "But that would give such a charming fillip of uncertainty, would it not? Like Russian roulette, an element of adventure and risk. Such an interesting gamble—a gamble you have not refused," he pointed out.

"I thought I had."

"Did she?" asked Baharian, appealing to his audience.

"Yes, but without conviction," said Lady Waring, amused.

Mr. Gunfer said coldly, "You're nothing but a rank opportunist, Baharian, you'd wear her like a boutonniere to feed your ego. What a cheap ego you have!"

"Or a large soul," mused Lady Waring.

"Stop—stop!" cried Miss Thorald, putting her hands over her ears. "It's impossible, you mustn't keep talking about it, I thank you, Mr. Baharian, I've enjoyed talking with you—"

"—and trust we may continue," he put in.

"—but please don't speak of this again."

"I obey," he said with a bow. "I have not spoken, the words are erased." Turning to Gen he said, "Small one, your eyes are as big as saucers, I fear I have distracted us from the business at hand, shall we continue? Or shall we talk instead of what great entertainment you will take back to your village when you return to it from Rangoon?"

Gen flushed, realizing the time had come when she must speak but the words stuck in her throat nevertheless. Straightening her shoulders and lifting her chin she told him, "I won't be going back to Theingyu, I'm to go on to America."

Six pairs of eyes swerved to her, five of them in surprise. Mrs. Caswell said doubtfully, "Are you being sent to America for schooling, is that it?"

But Lady Waring, watching Gen, shook her head. "No," she said quietly, "no, I don't believe that's it and I don't think we should pry further."

This was so unlike Lady Waring that five pairs of eyes swerved to regard her with surprise, too.

Gen said, "It's all right, you know. I mean, I have to practice saying it, that they're dead. My mother and father, I mean."

"Oh my dear," said Mrs. Caswell. "Both parents?"

"She doesn't need pity," said Lady Waring sharply. "She needs anger—it's anger that keeps people going."

"I wasn't offering her pity," Mrs. Caswell said impatiently.

"Tragedies don't interest me, tragedies and heartbreaks are all alike, what matters is how a person meets them, how they *survive* them. Given the inevitability of losses and disappointments in life, that's where the challenge is and the uniqueness. I was offering her sympathy."

"Helen," said Lady Waring, startled, "you continue to surprise me."

"When?" asked Mr. Gunfer, looking at Gen as if he saw her for the first time. "Both at once?"

Gen shook her head. "No, my father killed—my father was killed a few days ago so now I'm to go to an aunt in New York City."

Baharian, studying her face, said shrewdly, "And don't feel like talking about it yet, right?"

"If you don't mind, no," she told him shyly.

"So!" he said with a wry smile, "We have now collected two matters not to be spoken of, and me—I think it is time we return to our quarrels, don't you all agree?"

Late that night, unable to sleep, Lady Waring rose in the darkness and picked her way over the sleeping forms around her and wandered out to the temple step. Finding it already occupied she said, "Oh!" and turned to go, but hearing her Mr. Ba Sein said, "No, please, Lady Waring."

She joined him, noting ruefully that even here the sound of Mr. Gunfer's snoring competed with the shrilling of cicadas in the forest. The air had cooled; a sliver of half-moon hung in the sky and a lantern glowed in the window of the guard hut, carving a circle of gold in the darkness.

She must have sighed, for Mr. Ba Sein turned his head to observe her. He said, "You grow tired, Lady Waring?"

"There's a limit to how long one can sleep on a stone floor

131

night after night," she said ruefully. "And there are also—I admit—too many things to think about." She hesitated and then said frankly, "I am finding it very tedious—for the first time in many years—to think of anyone other than myself. Mr. Ba Sein, I would like to apologize for my rudeness to you when we first met. I am being forced to realize—naturally against my will," she said dryly, "that I have become a very disagreeable and arrogant woman."

"Have you?" he said politely.

She smiled at him. "You know it very well, Mr. Ba Sein . . . When I met Helen Caswell I dismissed her—no, condemned her—as a witless and boring woman, apologetic for her very existence, and I did not respond well at *all* to Mr. Baharian, whose heroic proportions now appear to conceal a heroic nature as well. It's unsettling and it's making me cross. I don't like change, even in my opinions; I find it threatening."

"To what?" asked Mr. Ba Sein with interest. "And why?"

"I'm in danger of losing my anger," she told him. "I need my anger, I have been *sustained* by anger, I can't imagine how I'd live without my anger, and now—"

Mr. Ba Sein chuckled. "You speak with such fierceness that I almost see you shaking your fist at the heavens in your rage."

"Heavens? If you mean God I am perhaps angriest of all at God," she said tartly. "I stopped believing in him on the day that I heard Eric had been killed."

"Oh?"

She nodded. "I demanded answers of him," she said. "I demanded explanations and comfort—I suppose even bitterness and sterility are prayers of a sort—but God was silent. What is one to conclude?" she said with irony. "God did not appear to me in a vision, I had no healing dreams, I experienced no sense of Eric being with me still. God was deaf."

Mr. Ba Sein smiled. "What a burden you people in the West place on God! In the East, in much of the world, as you no doubt realize, it is believed that we live many lives, returning to this earth again and again, bringing consequences and responsibilities with us from past lives to meet again and work through. The stream of experiences that we call 'good,' and those we call 'bad,' come to us not from God but from ourselves, from what we've been in the past and what we make of ourselves in the present. Earth is a learning ground, that's all."

She gave him a sharp glance. "I suppose you mean what Gen called kan and what in India is called karma—as you see, I am familiar with the words," she said with a sniff. "There are theosophists in England, and anthroposophists as well. Rather bizarre people, I might add, the women tend to wear woolen stockings and beads, and are very earnest."

Amused, he said, "Yes, and Mrs. Caswell is witless and boring, and Mr. Baharian no more than a large and untidy man."

She laughed in spite of herself. "Touché, Mr. Ba Sein . . . As a matter of curiosity do Buddhists believe in God?"

He said in his tranquil voice, "The Buddha has said that God is like a moon reflected in a thousand bowls of water."

"That sounds rather detached."

"Does it? You in the West paint life on such a small canvas, Lady Waring. We in the East see life as a long, *long* struggle toward perfect knowledge, a procession of souls given flesh to love, hate, kill, victimize, forgive, sow, reap, create and destroy, be sinners or saints until at last we break through our shells to the God inside of us." He shook his head. "But in only one lifetime?"

"Procession," she mused. "A procession in the dark, then, lighted only by a candle."

"And the candle," he said, "is God."

133

She sighed. "So we return to God again—I'd prefer to return to my anger, Mr. Ba Sein."

He nodded. "One feels it in you, yes."

"And what would I be without it when it's all that's fueled me?"

"Drop it and find out!" he said with a laugh.

They had been noticed by the guards, one of whom had left the hut to stand in the glow of the lantern and watch them. Pointing to him Mr. Ba Sein said, "We are making them uneasy, they need their sleep, too."

He rose to his feet and so did she, but she touched his arm, her voice serious. "You've not answered my question, Mr. Ba Sein, what would I be?"

"Emptied," he told her gently.

"Then I would be nothing."

"On the other hand," he said softly as they entered the temple, "on the other hand when a gourd is hollowed out it becomes empty and is of great use to the world *because* of its emptiness." And with a smile, "Good night, Lady Waring, I wish you a restful sleep now."

12

ALREADY THEIR DAYS had begun to have a dreamlike quality, blurred by the monotony and the tedium, the hours so alike, so long and so difficult to fill that only darkness and daylight defined their passing, and it seemed inconceivable that they had been confined to the temple for only a week. Each morning Gen went down to the river with a companion and checked for a note under the rock from Ba Tu. Grass and rods were found for the cloth puppets. The rice was brought at nine and again around six in the evening; Baharian did his laps in the compound each morning and afternoon. U Ba Sein and Gen planned their marionette show and while he taught her several of the great yokthe pwe stories she in turn taught words of Burmese to Mrs. Caswell and to Miss Thorald, who read *Vampire Love* and knitted, unraveled her knitting and began again. U Ba Sein meditated, Lady Waring read Emerson and went on to sample Lao-tse, and Mr. Gunfer made his way through Gen's book of crossword puzzles.

And they talked and they argued.

"What," asked Mr. Gunfer distastefully, "is a four-letter word for 'tootsies'?"

"Feet," said Baharian with authority.

"And a song entitled 'Oh, You Beautiful' what?"

" 'Doll,' " said Mrs. Caswell. Turning to Gen, "What do you want from your new life in America?"

"Want from life in America?" she repeated, puzzled. "That's what I would like. Life from America."

"I'll rephrase that," Mrs. Caswell said, smiling. "What do you look forward to, hope for, want for yourself?"

"Well," Gen told her earnestly, "U Ba Sein says this life is an important one for me and I want to learn what he means."

"I see," said Mrs. Caswell, giving U Ba Sein a quick, startled glance across the room. "This particular life, you mean, speaking from the—er—Buddhist viewpoint of many lives?"

With a nod, "Yes, I want to learn why I've lived in Burma, and why my mother died of typhoid seven years ago and my father last week. These matters are important to me."

"Philosophy," said Mrs. Caswell, nodding. "But I really don't think—"

"And at the end of my life," Gen said firmly, "I want—oh, to be a very wise person, like U Ba Sein."

"Not rich? Not happily married with many children?"

Gen brushed these aside with a wave of her hand. *"Wise.* I want—oh, I want that very much. But wisdom needs much living, so what I want—yes—is life in America."

Quite astonished by Gen's firmness, even by the passion with which she spoke, Mrs. Caswell was reduced to saying, "I see."

"And what," said Mr. Gunfer that evening, "is a five-letter word for a rich man?"

Baharian said, "Being a socialist you'd not know, I suppose. You did say you're a socialist?"

"Try 'nabob,' " suggested Mrs. Caswell, counting on her fingers.

"But a socialist turned prosperous," pointed out Lady Waring with sarcasm. "At least I assume such books as Cynthia Gore has written have made rather a lot of money."

Mr. Gunfer said with equal sarcasm, "Enough so that I could come to Burma and be captured by insurgents, yes."

"As a socialist I daresay your sympathies would lie with the insurgents then, Mr. Gunfer?"

He said stiffly, "I don't approve of their methods—"

"—not when they include you, of course, no."

"—but I certainly approve of their plans and dreams for making Burma a socialist country."

"Is that what they want?"

"From what I've heard and read, yes."

"So you're a Communist," she said accusingly.

"Not at all. Socialism," he told her, "is quite *quite* different, but not to your liking either, I'm sure, since in the distribution of wealth and land, Lady Waring, you would certainly have to share your fortune."

She sniffed. "What fortune? Since the war, England is a ravaged country with shortages of everything. I *cannot* believe this would have happened if Mr. Churchill was still our Prime Minister, it's been a great shock to me, the country turning to the Labor Party."

"I'll bet. How many castles have you had to sell?"

"No castles, Mr. Gunfer," she told him coldly, "but it's been necessary to sell a country home that's been in the family for generations."

"Country home," he said savagely. "May one inquire how many rooms in this 'country home'?"

Lady Waring hesitated, and Gen, accustomed now to battles waged, guessed that Mr. Gunfer was going to win this one, and she grinned. "Thirty rooms," said Lady Waring.

"Leaving you with—?"

"I will not be interrogated, Mr. Gunfer!"

"The shortages, the ravages, no doubt being only among the poor, Lady Waring. You suffer shock? In an ideal society you would have only *one* home, and everyone, Lady Waring," he said triumphantly, "would also have a home."

She rallied hotly. "In such a society, Mr. Gunfer, you would be writing tracts, not books of fiction that bring you money for trips abroad!"

"You speak like—"

"Oh dear, do please stop," cried Mrs. Caswell, and when both of them turned to glare at her, "I do so mind loud voices."

U Ba Sein intervened, saying gently, "This could perhaps be continued tomorrow for it grows very late and it is time, is it not, to sleep now?"

"I don't know why," grumbled Lady Waring, "when tomorrow will be exactly the same as today."

But the next day was not the same at all because in the morning Colonel Wang paid them his second visit, bringing with him harsh news. Initially his appearance was a welcome relief to Lady Waring because worry had increasingly begun to supplant her boredom and she was impatient for news. During their first hours and days of captivity she had pooh-poohed the delays that Colonel Wang had foreseen but he had made it all too clear what lay ahead if Rangoon proved unresponsive, and each day when Baharian made a mark in charcoal on the wall, denoting another day of imprisonment, her confidence—or had it been her arrogance, she wondered now—had grown a little less. This morning when a sliver of sun could be seen over the fence that blocked their view, and when Gen and Mr. Gunfer had gone under guard to the river to bring back water, she went out into the compound to find Baharian and tell him so.

"But yes," he had said, looking down at her with kind eyes. "Why do you think I stride so ridiculously around this compound twice a day? Soon I will have to begin running to quiet my thoughts, and for a man my size—"

"Perhaps we should be like Mr. Ba Sein," she said. "Nothing seems to worry him, but of course he doesn't *know,* you and Miss Thorald are the only ones who overheard Colonel Wang. *Should* we worry?" she asked him. "This is our eighth morning here, does this mean trouble, is it possible there is resistance in Rangoon to freeing us?"

"More likely some resistance to meeting all of Colonel Wang's demands," he said, and led her to the step of the temple and bid her sit down while he struggled into his shirt. "One must look at the bright side, Lady Waring: none of us has become ill from malaria, or from the water—"

"Yet," she said grimly.

"Mr. Gunfer has turned almost civil, and slowly we acquire a taste for cold rice—"

"Speak for yourself."

"The small one has offered to provide meat for us—"

"You mean catch rats with her slingshot," said Lady Waring with a shudder. "Is it really possible they ate them here during the war?"

"Anything is possible," he assured her. "I myself went ashore

139

in France shortly after D-Day and was pinned down for three days by mortar fire in a cellar without a crumb of food. One more day and—" He shrugged. "Who knows? We at least have rice to eat."

"Yes, tirelessly and tiresomely."

"And we can all look forward presently to being entertained by a marionette show."

"You have still not soothed my worries, Mr. Baharian."

"They are mine, too, Lady Waring. Ah—the water bearers return."

Watching Gen and Mr. Gunfer appear from behind the guard hut she said crossly, "Why does that girl volunteer now each morning to go down the hill and bring up water? It's a great deal too much for her, she's thin enough."

"The young do not like to be caged."

"The old do not like to be caged either," she said tartly.

Mr. Gunfer nodded to them, deposited a heap of grass on the earth and carried his bucket inside. Gen, looking discouraged, put down her bucket on the step, dropped a bundle of bamboo stems and began flexing her stiffened fingers. When Baharian said, "You look discouraged, small one," she managed a smile but it was feeble: there was still no message under the rock from Ba Tu, and she too wanted news.

It was now that Colonel Wang appeared, marching briskly across the compound accompanied by two satellites in shapeless khaki. "We have spoken of the devil, as the saying goes," said Baharian, "and now he arrives. Let us hope he comes as a saint, to tell us we are to be freed."

Colonel Wang gestured them into the temple as he passed, and the three of them followed. Inside, Miss Thorald had interrupted her reading of *Vampire Love* to light a fire, Mr. Gunfer was pouring water from his bucket into the kettle, and Mrs.

Caswell, eyes closed, was again reciting her numbers, *"Ti, hni, thoun, lei, nga, hcau . . ."* but upon hearing them she opened her eyes and rose nervously to her feet.

Gen said eagerly, "Are we *leitte?* Are we free?"

He ignored this. Folding his arms he looked them over, his eyes moving from one face to another. "You look well," he said with a nod. "Good—now I wish to check your names again." Bringing out a notebook he added, "You will tell me if any are in error . . . Lady Sara Waring, London, England . . . Helen F. Caswell, Phoenix, Arizona, U.S.A. . . . T. Baharian, San Francisco, California, U.S.A. . . . Calvin Gunfer, New Hope, Pennsylvania, U.S.A. . . . Lina T. Lerina, U.S.A., no other address given . . . Mr. Ba Sein of Rangoon."

"And now there's Gen," said Mrs. Caswell, pointing to her.

The colonel looked her over distastefully. "Last name?"

"Ferris."

But he neither wrote it down nor asked for a passport so that Gen felt she'd been rendered invisible and of no consequence, and she hated him for this. *A low Buddhist,* she thought, consigning him to Awizi, the nethermost hell, and hoped that her thamma deva would take note of this.

"And now," said Lady Waring firmly, "you will please tell us what is happening in Rangoon to delay our release."

He laughed. "You are not so valuable as you believed," he said, looking at Lady Waring and obviously entertained by this thought. "They have so far refused our demands."

"That's impossible," said Lady Waring.

"What *are* your demands?" asked Mr. Gunfer.

"They can't have refused all of them!" cried Mrs. Caswell.

"No? Our demands are not your business but I can tell you they are being ignored, which is very foolish of them because the rice we give you each day is taken from the mouths of my soldiers. Times are not good here, not even money can buy rice when there is none, and we cannot feed you much longer. My soldiers did not become soldiers to see their rice given to Europeans. A deadline has now been given to Rangoon."

They waited, eyes riveted on the colonel; a deadline did not sound attractive.

"We have given Rangoon forty-eight more hours," he said. "If our conditions are not—"

He stopped as one of his soldiers carried in their morning bucket of rice. Speaking sharply in Burmese he told him not to interrupt, to be silent, to wait, and when Gen gave the young man a sympathetic glance she saw that it was Ko Thein. *So he is back on duty,* she thought, but although she tried to catch his eye he hung his head and stared at the floor, as if in shame at being chastised by his superior; a second later Gen forgot him when she heard what the colonel said.

"I was saying that Rangoon has been given a deadline," he continued curtly. "If our conditions are not met in forty-eight hours—" He shrugged and his voice softened. "I am sorry but I have no choice in this matter, I cannot let you go free and I cannot go on feeding you."

"Meaning what?" faltered Mrs. Caswell.

"Meaning you will have to be executed . . . shot."

"Executed!" cried Mr. Gunfer.

"You'd *kill* us?" gasped Gen.

"Oh dear God," murmured Mrs. Caswell. "And what day is today?"

"Today is what you call Tuesday," he said crisply. "If there has been no action from Rangoon by Thursday morning at this hour—" He shrugged. "So be it."

Oh where is my thamma deva now, wondered Gen, her heart jumping as she thought how quickly Thursday would come. She turned to look for U Ba Sein and discovered that he was watching her—she was visible to him at least, and of consequence—but what did he see when he looked at her so closely? He had told her that her thamma deva had not abandoned her but how could she believe him when death was threatened in forty-eight hours and Ba Tu had not returned or left a message? And if she was to die, would she go to one of the four Buddha States of Punishment, to a Seat of the Nats, or would she go to the Christian heaven or hell?

Who am I, she cried silently, and in despair: *which? who? in what can I believe?*

U Ba Sein smiled at her, a smile so serene that it startled her, and into her thoughts flowed the words he'd spoken earlier: *you will be, still, a visitor from the stars.* These words steadied her, she straightened her shoulders and her chin went up, she smiled shyly back at U Ba Sein and returned her attention to Colonel Wang.

He was leaving now, cutting off their protests, their demands that more time be given Rangoon, the deadline postponed, that they be allowed to send messages of their own to Rangoon. With a curt nod he beckoned to Ko Thein, who deposited the rice in their kettle, and with sadness Gen watched Ko Thein follow the colonel out of the temple without even a glance at her. Hopeless, she thought, absolutely hopeless, Ba Tu would bring help too late, they would all have been killed and she would never see America, or dress like the girls in the magazine. Or learn to dance or see a real motion picture or wear new shoes . . .

There was silence and then Mr. Gunfer gasped, "But I don't want to die in forty-eight hours!"

"We must remain calm," said Baharian.

"Speak for yourself," Lady Waring told him crossly, "I may

be sixty-eight but I'm not prepared to go yet, I've an appointment at a village in Upper Burma."

"Of course this isn't unexpected," Mrs. Caswell said slowly, "I just didn't believe it could happen so soon."

"You continue to surprise me," said Lady Waring, but her tone was sarcastic now.

"I don't know why," replied Mrs. Caswell. "Harry and I have been in a good many tight spots. Angry natives who think we're desecrating ancestral graves, political coups that send us flying just ahead of screaming rebels—"

Her voice was so prosaic that it had a soothing effect on anyone inclined to hysteria but it did not discourage Mr. Gunfer from saying bitterly, "Except that we can't fly away from *here.*"

Oh we must, thought Gen, *we* must *escape, there has to be some way,* and echoing her thought Baharian said, "We *must* escape, there has to be a way."

"Our man of action," said Lady Waring tartly.

"How?" cried Gen.

Baharian shrugged. "This we must speak of, but it seems to me—" He frowned. "Surely if we are to be killed by them in forty-eight hours it would be kinder to die trying to escape."

Mr. Gunfer made a face. "Horrible thought, but you're right, it gives us choice."

Miss Thorald nodded. "Yes, a choice of how and when."

"Thank you for agreeing, my dear," said Baharian, giving her a smile. "I told you we would have prospered together."

"Mr. Baharian, Terry—"

"We could rush the gate," broke in Mrs. Caswell. "That's the word for it, isn't it? After all, there are only two guards and seven of us."

"Two guards with loaded rifles," put in Mr. Gunfer.

144

"How about crawling past the guard hut in the middle of the night, does anyone know if they ever sleep on duty?"

"At night," said Mr. Ba Sein quietly, "there are always two guards, and very late in the night, when we are quiet and if one of them wishes to sleep, he comes to the step of the temple and lies down there."

Baharian said in surprise, "You've seen this?"

Mr. Ba Sein nodded. "Yes, I need very little sleep and it is sometimes pleasant to sit outside and look at the stars."

Mr. Gunfer said thoughtfully, "We have matches and live embers, what if we set fire to the fence outside and made a dash for it?"

"I doubt it would burn fast enough for us to escape through it and certainly any fire would be noticed at once."

"Nevertheless," began Baharian, and stopped, seeing that one of the guards was standing by the pillar, face impassive.

Mrs. Caswell whispered, "Has he been listening? How much has he heard?"

But Gen, trembling, stood up because it was Ko Thein; he had come back. She waited uncertainly for his eyes to find her, and when they did he curved a beckoning finger.

Lady Waring, seeing this, cried harshly, *"Don't go!* You . . . what do you want with her?"

"It's all right," cried Gen, racing to his side. "Ko Thein?"

In a low voice he said, *"Ba Tu, la neide."*

"Bedo?" she asked.

"Sei nya."

A dozen questions hammered at Gen but Ko Thein placed a finger to his lips, backed away and hurried out of the temple.

"What is it?" asked Mr. Gunfer.

Soberly, frowning over it, Gen said, "He has told me that Ba Tu is coming—before night."

"What on earth are you talking about?" asked Lady Waring. In a kinder voice Baharian said, "Who or what is Ba Tu?"

"My friend," she said simply, and told them of how Ba Tu had returned her father's gold watch to her, and of how he had come to the gate of the compound to speak to her four days ago.

"But why didn't you tell us?" demanded Lady Waring.

"I feared you would be heard talking of it, and there was also the fear he might not find boats."

"A dacoit!" echoed Mr. Gunfer incredulously.

"Do you think he's found boats now?" asked Miss Thorald. "Do you think he's heard about Colonel Wang's ultimatum?"

"I don't know," Gen said helplessly. "I don't know if he's found boats, I don't know anything, not even when he will come, or if he'll get through to us. It will be dangerous for him to come by daylight. If he's caught—" She shivered. "You see how it is."

"But still there begins to be a hope," said Mrs. Caswell.

"Hope is a beautiful word," said Baharian, "but we must not hope too much or expect too much. What we must do—there was to be a marionette show, was there not? It is now—" He looked at his watch. "It is now ten o'clock in the morning, a long day ahead of us, and I think we must become extremely busy and complete the small one's puppets. You agree, Mr. Ba Sein?"

Mr. Ba Sein smiled.

"You joke, surely!" cried Mr. Gunfer. "Puppets, after this?"

"Puppets," Baharian told him firmly. "One thinks better when busy, and if this Ba Tu doesn't reach us by night we must have plans. In the meantime we have rods now for the puppets, and only one head left to complete, and dear God but we also have long hours ahead that can easily drive us mad. To be torn between hope and despair—I have been there, it is not good territory."

"When?" asked Miss Thorald curiously. "Where?"

"The war."

"I loathe suspense," complained Mr. Gunfer. "My God I loathe suspense, I just hope my heart is strong enough to sustain it."

"I'm quite familiar with it," said Miss Thorald with asperity, "and I can assure you that you'll live through it."

"Unless of course we die at the end of it," pointed out Lady Waring, and realized there were tears in her eyes. *How humiliating,* she thought, *I've lived with death for so long and lost so many to death, why can't I accept that it will happen to me, too?* She rose and walked unsteadily to the doorway and stood looking out into the sunbaked compound, furious at the ugly fence that prevented her from seeing the river. She needed a river: the sight of water had always calmed her, it was why she so dearly loved Cornwall. She thought, *It's so undignified to be this stubborn about letting go,* and she closed her eyes, imagining the river as life, moving from brook to ocean, birth to death, and herself at its edge, clinging desperately to a tree, a bush, a tuft of grass, struggling to hold back while the river flowed tranquilly past, mocking her.

Gen had followed her. She said anxiously, "Are you all right?"

The moment passed, the tears dried. Lady Waring said gruffly, "Watch out or I'll stop scolding you for your impertinence, Gen Ferris." To the others she called, "Well, where are you? You heard Mr. Baharian, we've work to do!"

But there was not enough work for seven people and it was hot outside in the compound, and attention was spasmodic. Gen thought, *Suddenly they're all actors, pretending to be interested, to be cheerful, and every hour that passes they can't help but give me accusing glances because nothing happens.* But she was a captive of suspense too, wanting very much to speak with U Ba Sein, who appeared to go to unusual lengths to avoid speech with her. She would say anxiously, "U Ba Sein—"

And he would interrupt to say, "The prince will sing the song from the *Zawtagomma pyazat,* I think . . . and I believe that much as it shatters all traditions we must give him a mustache like a European or he will look exactly like the princess." And with a piece of charcoal from the fire he would study the cloth head and make a tentative line.

"But U Ba Sein—"

"Tomorrow we will practice hard," he said, as if not hearing her. "We must practice all day and present our performance before Colonel Wang returns so that we continue to live with intention."

She could only turn back to the others, who spoke now of finding a way to scale the high fence, although Mrs. Caswell still clung to the idea of rushing the guards, rifles or not. By three o'clock in the afternoon, hot and tired, they drifted back into the temple's shaded coolness to hug their particular fears and to go over and over new ideas for escape. Only Gen remained outside, sitting on the step of the temple in a patch of shade.

She was discouraged and she was depressed, for Ko Thein had been absent from the compound for several hours and he had been replaced by two new guards; she could only stare fixedly at the guard hut and will Ba Tu to find a way to get through to her, but no shadow appeared, the guards lazed in the shade of the fence without concern, the afternoon was on the wane and there was no Ba Tu.

Ba Tu, la neide . . . When, she had asked . . . *Before night,* Ko Thein had said.

Oh, Ba Tu, she prayed, *you have seven lives in the palm of your hand, come to us, don't abandon us . . .*

It was not good to be abandoned; she separated the word from the others and considered it, and then she brought out her feelings about the word, recognizing them from her mother's death, and again from her father's death, and for a moment she experienced a death of her own as she sat on the step and saw and understood how alone she was in the world now. Alone, she thought, alone *alone,* testing the word, and then through her tears her eyes caught a flutter of movement off to the left. She saw that a butterfly had attached itself to one of the few sheaths of grass that Mr. Gunfer had overlooked; it lingered a moment and then with a twinkle of wings fluttered closer, brushed her arm and to her surprise settled fearlessly on her knee.

She held her breath.

Its wings were a vivid shade of blue like the sky at noon on a cloudless day, and each was outlined in brilliant shades of red with a slash of gold inside the scarlet. She marveled at it, for in all of her nearly seventeen years in this country she had never seen or heard of a butterfly such as this, and had certainly never met one so bold.

She thought, *It's a sign . . .*

Perhaps she had not been forgotten, after all. Or abandoned.

The wings quivered, the butterfly rose and fluttered away, hovered over a stem of grass and then flew upward to vanish over the fence and melt into the blue of the sky, leaving Gen its butterfly image forever.

Behind her Miss Thorald cleared her throat. "I realized you're still out here and I don't think you should be by yourself just now." Seating herself on the broad step next to Gen she

149

said softly, "Have you faced death before, Gen? You were here during the war, weren't you?"

It needed a strenuous effort to shift her attention to Miss Thorald. "Yes—yes we were here," she said, blinking away the last of her tears, and then, realizing what Miss Thorald meant, "But I suppose it's different to know exactly when it can happen —like now, if Ba Tu doesn't come, or if he comes to say he can't help us." She added clumsily, "I daresay when we're born someone knows exactly when we'll die, but we don't."

Miss Thorald reached for Gen's hand, squeezed it lightly and released it. "We're all a little crazy today, I think—like that bird shrieking at us from the woods."

"It's a cuckoo," Gen told her, so impressed by Miss Thorald's quick warm gesture, a gesture that seemed to remove the years and the experience between them, that she said, "Will you have been sorry you said no to Mr. Baharian's proposal? Do you like him?"

"He's certainly different from anyone I've ever known," said Miss Thorald. "Yes I like him—he's a very surprising person."

Gen nodded. "Lady Waring keeps saying that about Mrs. Caswell, too."

Miss Thorald smiled. "There seem to be many surprises, don't there . . . I can't tell you how different everyone was on the steamer, in spite of being thrown together for seven days, and the only nonnatives aboard. Lady Waring had her secretary with her, and a man assigned her from the consulate named Culpepper, and she was very haughty and distant. Mrs. Caswell was nice but inseparable from her husband; Mr. Gunfer was condescending, and Mr. Baharian—well, his exuberance and his friendliness were considered brash, I think. Somehow it was all so polite and cool and formal."

"So they were wearing masks," said Gen triumphantly, feeling that her point was proved.

Miss Thorald nodded. "I think you're right. I wonder . . . yes, I wonder if we can ever really know a person until we know them under stress. Gen, that is a *very* noisy bird!"

Gen had already tensed; it was not only an unusually noisy cuckoo but it had moved closer, repeating over and over its wild insane cry. She whispered, "Oh Miss Thorald," and rose to her feet. "Miss Thorald, that has to be Ba Tu. Where is it coming from, it's a signal!"

Miss Thorald said calmly, "From behind the latrine, I believe."

"In broad daylight, too," whispered Gen.

"I'll cover for you," said Miss Thorald. "One of the guards is watching, pretend you're using the latrine. Be careful!"

"Yes," said Gen and walked to the hole in the ground and squatted over it, calling in a low voice, "Ba Tu?"

It was Ba Tu.

"Have you heard?" she whispered. *"Ame,* in forty-eight hours they will kill us if nothing's heard from Rangoon!"

"Sssh, I've heard," he said, his mouth pressed to the fence. "It's what brought me back. Be very quiet and listen, Zen—it has to be tonight."

"You found boats?"

"No boats . . . boats yes, but not here, Zen, ten miles downstream. There wasn't time, there's been time for nothing, but Bo Gale and I, we have made a *poun."*

"What plan?"

"For tonight, after they've brought your evening rice and when the stars are out but not yet the moon."

"Na male bu."

"We have a digging tool," he explained. "We stole it, a

151

shovel, it was all we could think of. We'll dig a *twin*—a hole in the ground—here, under this fence, in this place, Zen. And you will crawl under and run, all of you."

"They'll hear you!" she protested.

"Yes, so you must find a way to make noise, much noise, for about *leize* minutes—forty minutes—because we will have to creep on stomachs to this place and then dig a big hole. You must make large noises, Zen, pretend someone's sick. Scream, yell, cry. Go crazy."

"Ssst, a guard's coming!" hissed Miss Thorald.

"Yatte," Gen told Ba Tu, "a guard is coming."

The guard was new and he was young and conscientious, and he took his assignment to guard the Europeans seriously. From across the compound he had heard mumbling from this thin girl with the hat but although he closely watched her companion, the older woman, he had not seen her lips move in reply; he wanted now to know to whom the thin one was speaking. *"Hei,"* he demanded, "who do you talk with?"

Gen was ready for him; she looked up and said crossly, "I'm practicing words for our puppet show, one does that even at the toilet. I'm going over and over the words I will say, to memorize them."

"Puppet show? What puppet show?" he asked skeptically.

"We're giving one tomorrow," she told him, and added carelessly, "You guards may watch if you'd like. Or maybe," she said, seized by inspiration, "maybe we'll give the show *tonight*—yes, tonight. Miss Thorald," she called to her, "we had really planned to give the show tonight, hadn't we?"

"Of course," said Miss Thorald demurely.

"You see? Now go away, it's not polite for you to stand there."

He retreated, calling out to his fellow guard the news of

prisoners crazy enough to give a show for them, and once he had distanced himself Gen giggled. "You heard, Ba Tu? We will give a show, a very noisy one. We'll ask to use their hut by the gate for the show, and make sure their backs are turned to the latrine. After the rice—you will see them bring the rice?"

"We'll see, yes," Ba Tu said. "And we'll wait for noise."

"Be careful, Ba Tu."

"You too, Zen. Make it *very* loud!"

She heard the rustle of palm leaves behind the fence and then silence. Gen stood up, beamed at Miss Thorald, and together they went in to tell the others what lay ahead for them in only a few hours.

The butterfly had truly been a sign.

13

IT WAS MR. BA SEIN who undertook to discuss with the guards the borrowing of their hut, with its window looking out on the compound. With their permission, he explained courteously, he and Zen might stand behind the window and operate the puppets they'd made during the past few days, with the audience seated on the ground below the window, and if the guards wished to invite friends they would have a very merry yokthe pwe. A short tale, of course, and the puppets were primitive but he was a puppetmaster who knew all the stories and the songs, and he thought they might enjoy it, too. Very gently he insinuated that the colonel need not be told about this, since it would be a very modest show at which the colonel might sneer, coming from another country, and would a lantern and a few extra candles be possible?

Mr. Gunfer, looking haggard, said, "This is even worse,

154

there begins to feel something more comfortable about being shot to death. What if we're seen or heard escaping? And we'll have to run, won't we? What if one of us can't run fast enough?"

"Or trips and falls—or has an appendicitis attack," said Baharian with humor. "Come, come, Gunfer, we're to be rescued by dacoits—brigands, bandits! Here is fat material for your next book."

"How dare you," said Mr. Gunfer but he said it weakly, so that it could be seen from the narrowing of his eyes that he was considering this suspense from a new angle and had been neatly diverted after all.

Gen and Mr. Ba Sein had taken over the corner next to the archway and were devising a plot for the show, elaborating on it and memorizing it. "We must stretch the story like a rubber band," he told her. "You can do this, Zen? We must fill time, say many words where one word might do."

Gen nodded nervously; it was useless to say that she would try to do this, she *must* do it. "I could begin by telling a folk tale before the show starts," she said. "One of the Boatmen stories maybe?"

"Capital idea," he cried warmly, and patted her approvingly on the shoulder. "And I will choose the longest songs that I know, even if—" He smiled. "Even if stolen from another tale, which is most unprofessional!"

After this it was necessary to wait, and to listen to the pounding of their hearts while each of them, and Lady Waring in particular, worried about racing for their lives over untilled earth in the darkness, worried as to how soon their absence might be discovered if they got away, and how organized a pursuit would be.

Lady Waring said, "The time will drag now and then sud-

155

denly it will move too quickly. I am a connoisseur of time, and it never behaves as one wishes."

"When actually time exists only in the mind," said Mr. Ba Sein with a smile.

"What's in *your* mind?" she asked, genuinely curious.

"The words I will sing for the prince tonight; I have not sung them for a long time."

"But don't you present marionette shows every week at your Jubaliho theater?"

"A puppetmaster is always busy—here and there," he said vaguely, and turned away to adjust the rod on one of the puppets.

The sun moved across the sky and met the horizon, and the shafts of light high up near the temple ceiling grew dim. They lighted their usual evening fire for warmth, and when the rice was brought the guards carried with them the two lanterns they had promised for the performance, and a fresh supply of candles. They ate quickly, their hunger outweighing fear and suspense for that moment, and when the rice kettle was empty they carried it out and placed it inside the guard hut to hit and thump for sound effects. The sky in the east held a slash of crimson at the horizon but it was a brief twilight and faded swiftly.

Seven guards filtered in through the gate, grinning self-consciously as they joined the two on duty; they seated themselves on the ground facing the guard hut, their backs to the temple and to the latrine while Mr. Gunfer, Lady Waring and Mrs. Caswell took places behind them.

Baharian lit the two lanterns . . . It was time to begin.

Walking to the front of the hut Gen smiled, bowed and announced in a very loud voice that before the performance began she would tell the story of *The Boatman and the Boatmaster,* and she would tell it in both English and Burmese.

Baharian, having seated himself in the rear, shouted "Bravo!" and led the others in applause, the guards laughing at Baharian's enthusiasm. In the hut behind her U Ba Sein pounded on the kettle with two sticks, producing a drum roll, and when he subsided, Gen began.

"This," she said, "is the story of a boatmaster who was so greedy that he would cheat his own workers of their wages, and because a journey up and down the Irrawaddy lasted for several months their wages came to quite a sum. This boatmaster gave his men food during the trip but for their time and work the payment came on the last day when the journey had been finished, and on this last day—every time—the boatmaster would play a trick or challenge his men to a bet, and the more innocent or trusting of his men would end up being cheated out of their entire two or three months' wages."

Here she stopped to translate her words into Burmese, and the soldiers, who already knew and loved the story, nodded and grinned.

"On this particular trip," she went on, "there was a new man called Chan. On the last day of their voyage they stopped at a village. It was January and the water was icy cold and the boatmaster said, 'I wonder if there is anyone among you hardy enough to stay in the water all night long, without clothes on, and without anything to warm him. If one of you boatmen can stay in the water all night I'll give him all my boats. But if he fails to stay in the water until dawn, he loses all his wages. How's that for a fair bet?' "

"Speak louder," called Baharian from the rear, and Gen, who had been close to shouting, drew a deep breath and shouted louder, "Since all the boatmen were strong and hardy men they might have accepted the bet but they had already been warned about their master's tricks and so they said nothing." She

157

stopped, and with a grin at Mr. Baharian called, "Can you hear me now?"

"Yes," he shouted, grinning back at her.

With a nod she went on. "But Chan," she shouted, "was a new boatman and he was also stubborn and he thought he could outsmart this master and win the bet. So he stripped off his clothes and went into the water . . . His teeth chattered and his body shivered from the cold but—he stayed. He stayed in the icy water and the hours passed and now it was nearly dawn."

She paused a moment for effect, experiencing the heady effect of an audience hanging on her every word. "And then," she continued in her loudest voice, "just as the boatmaster had known would happen—because it happened every single day at this village—some fishermen on the other side of the river got up out of their beds and made a fire in front of their hut to warm themselves before going out fishing. When their fire was burning brightly on the opposite bank the boatmaster cried out, 'Boatman, you are cheating. You are taking advantage of the fire across the river on the opposite bank and so you've lost the bet by default.' 'But the fire is on the other side of the river,' protested Chan. 'It's surely half a mile away, how can it give me any warmth?'

"To this the boatmaster said, 'A fire is a fire and as long as it's visible it gives you warmth. You have lost the bet and you have lost all your wages.'

"Very cheerfully Chan shrugged, said 'All right' and climbed out of the water." And here she translated what she had just spoken into Burmese for any of the soldiers who had not been taught English.

"So," she continued, her voice cracking a little at being lifted to such volume, "so the boatman Chan left the water and after dressing he went to sit with his fellow boatmen. He said, 'You probably think me a fool because I have lost my wages but if I'm a fool in other matters I can tell you that at least in pig roasting I have no equal. Even our clever boatmaster doesn't know how to roast pig's trotters the right way.'

"Now the boatmaster was feeling pleased with himself, and he didn't like hearing that he wasn't clever enough to roast pig's trotters. 'Just see how I won your wages from you,' he said, 'and yet you say I don't know how to roast pig's trotters. Of course I know how!'

"Chan shook his head. 'Not pig's trotters, no. Maybe other meat but not pig's trotters.'

" 'Of course I know how,' shouted the boatmaster, growing angry, 'and I'll accept any bet about this to show you!'

" 'All right—I have some pig's trotters with me right now,' replied Chan, 'which I bought from a market boat yesterday, and I will give them to you to roast now. If you can roast them —why, I will serve you as a slave for seven years. If you fail, you must give me all your boats. That is a fair bet, and if you really think you can roast pig's trotters you ought to accept it.'

" 'I accept the bet,' said the boatmaster.

"Chan went and fetched the pig's trotters and said, 'Here they are. Now roast them.'

" 'But where is the fire?' asked the boatmaster.

"Chan said very sweetly, 'There is a fire on the shore across the river.'

" 'But that's half a mile away,' protested the boatmaster angrily.

"Chan shrugged. 'A fire is a fire—as you explained to me— and if it was hot enough to warm me in the water it is surely hot enough for you to roast pig's trotters. Now I see that you don't know how to roast them at all, so I've won the bet.'

"The boatmaster was so furious that when they reached the end of their journey he took this to a court of law but the judge ruled in Chan's favor, and so Chan became a boatmaster and the boatmaster was left with none."

The story ended, U Ba Sein pounded the kettle, the soldiers clapped, Gen bowed and shouted, "And now we start our yokthe pwe . . . !"

And so it began, with art sacrificed to noise, and accuracy to melodrama. The head of the first puppet appeared in the window—it was the prince—and U Ba Sein's obviously melodic voice turned into a loud roar as he sang the prince's song:

> Ah, cruel spite,
> Ah, cursed night,
> That tore my love away
> More comfort here
> In jungle drear
> Than in the golden day.

The ogre's head appeared, bringing cries of delight from the soldiers and a fanfare of kettle thumping. His head was wrapped in dark blue silk that gleamed in the light of the lanterns, and having contributed a portion of his shirt for the ogre, Mr. Gunfer had also contributed the idea of inserting thorns from a thorn tree into the fabric so that the ogre bristled with hair and had a fearsome aura. Adopting the dirgelike wails of her earlier adventure with U Hamlin, Gen uttered sinister moanings:

> The fog's death-cloud,
> Hangs like a shroud,
> Upon the shagg'd hillside;
> The tall trees mope,

The wild beasts grope
Now know what may betide . . .

The prince vanished, leaving the ogre alone in the window, and Lady Waring, seated at a distance, thought, *This is incredible and extremely hard to believe . . . I am sitting here in the dust next to an ancient temple located on the Irrawaddy River thousands of miles from home, it's night and I am watching this crazy, wild, lovable, absolutely insane and very noisy performance while behind the latrine two men—dacoits, no less!—are digging a hole to free us—or so we hope!—before we are all killed by insurgents in another's day time, and* —here she paused to loudly shout with the others as the ogre departed and the princess appeared—*and why,* she thought, *do I feel like laughing my head off?*

In a very unprincesslike voice Gen was shouting:

The wind breathes chill
Across the rill
    That cuts the forest track
    The haze to mist
    And I am lost, alack.

But the princess' charcoal eyebrows had disappeared, giving her an alarming leer, and Lady Waring's shoulders began to shake: she could no longer repress her feelings. Mercifully covered by the unholy bellowing from the stage, Lady Waring's laughter exploded at last, filling her, consuming her, radiating through her and—*how strange,* she thought, *I've not felt so alive since Matthew . . .*

Now the princess was cowering before the ogre, there was grave danger and a new song, and then—miraculously— Zawgwi appeared in the window of the hut, flying down from above to confront the ogre. There was talk, and a boisterous song; Zawgwi's wand was lifted and a spell was cast; the balu cried out, groaned and vanished below the sill. At this the prince reappeared and bellowed a rapturous song at finding his princess, and presently their two heads came together in what had to be assumed was an embrace. When they had disappeared, Zawgwi remained to sing of their love and of the story's conclusion; to walk, bow, shrug and gesture with all of U Ba Sein's skill and artistry—their one true puppet—and then he, too, vanished.

"And now," cried Gen, walking out of the hut, "our story ends!" And she bowed.

Baharian, checking his watch in the light of a lantern, nodded to her: forty-five minutes had passed. As he led the applause, with added shouts of Bravo, Mr. Ba Sein emerged from the hut and tactfully extinguished the two lanterns to discourage their guests from lingering. Slowly the soldiers rose, smiled at Gen and filed out of the gate, leaving behind only their two guards.

Gen gathered up Zawgwi and her shoulder bag, looked at U Ba Sein and said, "Well?"

"Yes," he said with a warm smile and a nod, and this was all the praise that Gen needed.

And now another show begins, she thought, and she turned to look at the temple, its bulk silhouetted against the starry night sky, its archway faintly defined by the glow of the charcoal fire burning inside. It was by plan that she and U Ba Sein lingered a moment with the pair of guards, engaging their attention so that it would not be noticed that five people veered off into the shadows at the side of the temple instead of passing through its dimly lighted doorway. U Ba Sein spoke with them for a moment, bid them a good night, and he and Gen headed for the temple, which they would enter and promptly leave again on hands and knees.

162

Lady Waring was the first to step over the latrine, drop to the ground and discover that yes, there really was a hole dug under the fence. As she squeezed through and came out into high grass that tickled her nose a low voice said, *"Go—Go!"* Guided by an unseen hand she stumbled away from the fence toward a nearby copse of trees. Miss Thorald was the second to burrow under the fence, followed by Mrs. Caswell and Mr. Gunfer. *"Myan! Myan!* Faster!" whispered Ba Tu.

On the other side Baharian whispered back, "I wait for Gen, the small one, and—ah, they come, they are here!" and Gen and U Ba Sein were hurried through the opening. Last of all came Baharian, but because his proportions had not been described to Ba Tu the hole was Burmese size and it became necessary to drag him through on his stomach, with U Ba Sein and Ba Tu each pulling one arm.

Quickly Ba Tu tossed handfuls of earth back into the hole, jumped up and rushed them toward the trees where Bo Gale waited, holding out a rope to which they must cling. Grasping this they were led in single file through the darkness down the hill toward the road. The moon rising in the east was as yet only a brush stroke of silver in the sky; an owl hooted mournfully at their passage, answered by a mynah bird, and then the forest stilled. Reaching the side of the road they stopped and waited, listening. From here, looking south, Gen could see the hillock from which an eternity ago she and U Hamlin had looked over a village that she had naively believed to be safe . . . *How long ago that was,* she thought.

Abruptly Ba Tu signaled them to go, and they were rushed like a herd of small animals across the road into the healing shadows of a forest.

14

THEY WERE ENTERING the world of the dacoit now and they moved without sound, guided by the rope and by the shadows of the two men with rifles who led them in and out of groves of bamboo and stands of palm and teak. Gen walked just behind Ba Tu and with every step her spirits rose to a new level of exhilaration. She was not only freed at last but she was with Ba Tu, who represented home to her and Ma Nu and Htun Schwae and U San Ya and—this, too—her father, so that she felt sheltered by the embrace of familiar trees and by Ba Tu's loyalty. Nor was she unacquainted with forest and jungle for when she was new to Theingyu, a mere eleven years of age, she and Ba Tu and Mi-Mi, Aung Maung and Chan Tu had made frequent forays into the woods to pick acacia leaves for betal, or thanaka bark to grind into paste for the girls' complexions. Even now she could vividly remember the evening she'd returned home with circles of creamy-white daubed on her cheeks; she could recall the sharpness of her father's voice when he ordered her to scrub it off at once. "You're not Burmese," he'd told her. "Thanaka's for natives, remove it." "But I'm a native—I live here," she'd protested. He had stared at her and then turned away with a curiously helpless gesture, as if understanding for the first time that she'd never experienced any culture but this one that to him was so alien. Nevertheless she'd quickly scrubbed away the thanaka, not wanting to ever see him look that way again.

Now she would have liked to ask Ba Tu why they were heading east toward the hills when he had said the boats waited for them ten miles to the south, on the river, but there was no way to confront him and ask; silence was imperative and so she gripped Zawgwi and her shoulder bag and obeyed the silence that was broken only by the keening of the cicadas or the raucous cries of a bird. The moon had risen high enough to drop small coins of silver light across the forest floor; Ba Tu had set a fast pace and behind her Gen could hear Lady Waring breathing heavily. After fifteen minutes of flight they stopped and stood waiting for another tug of the rope to signal advance.

"What is it?" whispered Mr. Gunfer.

In the distance a mynah bird chattered peevishly and subsided; a cuckoo laughed insanely. They had paused in the deep gloom of a bamboo grove but Gen could see diamonds of light beyond it that suggested an end to the forest and a savannah or cleared space ahead. The rope jerked again and they continued threading their way among the bamboo culms until they emerged into moonlight at the very edge of the forest.

The woods through which they had fled stood on higher ground than what lay below them, and they looked out over a broad expanse of flat and checkered fields. The moon hung low

in the purple sky, shedding a milky illumination. An owl hooted
dolorously behind them, a mynah gave a solitary cry but the
drone of cicadas had muted. A mile away Gen could see the
thread of dusty road that randomly followed the course of the
Irrawaddy on its way north to Mandalay, or south to Pagan and
Magwe. As her eyes lingered on the road she saw sudden movement and a small black shape catapulted into view followed by
clouds of dust, followed by a second identical shape, and Gen
said, "Look," and pointed.

"Jeeps," whispered Ba Tu.

"Government jeeps?" said Mr. Gunfer.

"Here? I do not think so."

"Why?"

Ba Tu said simply, "Because Ko Thein told me the Red Flags
had captured three jeeps last week, with petrol enough to fill
two."

Baharian said uneasily, "We shouldn't be stopping, should
we? We've been walking only"—he held his wristwatch to the
light—"a scant twenty minutes."

"We stop," said Ba Tu.

"But why?" asked Mrs. Caswell.

"Because there is danger, we think they are somewhere behind us."

" 'They'?" echoed Lady Waring sharply. "Who's behind us?"

"So soon?" gasped Mrs. Caswell.

"You mean already they know we're gone?"

"Ba Tu, how do you know this?" asked Gen.

He said evenly, "From the mynah bird and the cuckoo. Chi
Ti stayed behind to watch and to warn if we were seen or followed; he walks behind us now, twice he has sent a danger
signal—those were his calls—and now a signal to stop."

This was depressing news and Lady Waring slumped to the

ground, followed by Mrs. Caswell. Gen's exhilaration at their freedom faltered but she was not yet afraid. "How could they know we've gone?" she protested. "They've never entered the temple at night. Could the guards have heard us leave, or seen us?"

"And we were so quiet!" put in Mr. Gunfer.

"Perhaps," suggested U Ba Sein in his tranquil voice, "perhaps it is because of the performance that we gave. There may have been something we left behind and they decided to return it and found us gone."

"Oh dear," sighed Mrs. Caswell. "We were too friendly at the wrong time, then?"

"*Tashei*—please—sit and rest, we know nothing until Chi Ti comes to tell us," Ba Tu told them. "Bo Gale has gone back to cover our trail, to mend broken branches and torn leaves. If there is no danger we move on, so rest. As for me—" He stepped apart from them, tilted his head, opened his mouth and produced the wild strident cry of a cuckoo.

They waited.

"Can we talk now?" asked Baharian in a low voice.

"Yes."

"You carry an M1 carbine," said Baharian. "If there's trouble have you ammunition for it?"

"Some."

"How many rounds?"

Ba Tu shifted uneasily. "Two."

Baharian stared at him in horror. "That's all? What about the others?"

"It is Bo Gale who has the two rounds," said Ba Tu. "This rifle—mine—is empty."

Mr. Gunfer groaned.

"Empty!" gasped Miss Thorald.

167

Ba Tu said with dignity, "I am not a *sitta* or a *sipbou*. I may be a *damya*—a dacoit—but I am also Buddhist and I do not take life. I promised this, to the Buddha and to ame, my mother, who Gen calls Ma Nu."

"Well that's that, then," said Baharian, nodding. "What about your friend who has the two bullets in his magazine, does he feel the same way?"

Ba Tu shrugged. "This you will have to ask him. There has never been any shooting. We have so far stolen"—he thought about this—"one jeep, two jeep motors, many rubber tires, shoes, a lorry full of bananas, a load of cloth and some gold. But never has there been a need for shooting."

Baharian said dryly, "It's up to us bloodthirsty Westerners then."

"But not before we thank Ba Tu for rescuing us," Lady Waring said warmly. "We thank you, Ba Tu."

Mrs. Caswell nodded vigorously. "Much *kutho* for you!"

Ba Tu showed his pleasure at this with a broad grin that quickly faded. Lifting a hand he said, "Ssssh . . . someone is near."

The others had heard nothing but they had not lived by their wits as dacoits did, thought Gen, knowing strange hiding places and trails in the forest. She herself had keener ears than her companions, having lived in a country village and she had already noticed the sudden stillness in the forest behind them: even the *bazin yinkhwe* had stopped their shrilling. Poised between the darkness behind them and the milky light beyond them they waited with some nervousness and then a twig snapped, there was a rustle of tall grass, and Chi Ti emerged.

He arrived breathless, looking even younger to Gen than he had looked when he'd robbed her and U Hamlin in another forest on another night. He was in panic, his words tumbling out so quickly that Gen, who still thought in English, could not follow what he said.

"What is it?" she cried at last, interrupting.

Ba Tu translated in a sober, troubled voice. "We were seen crossing the road by a sentry far from where we crossed. It is too bad that Colonel Wang was in the village preparing a morning attack on the village south of us."

"South!" said Gen. "That's where we go."

"We hoped, yes," said Ba Tu grimly. "You foreign ones matter much more, it seems, for the colonel—ame, he is angry, Chi Ti lay in the grass and heard him—the colonel has sworn to have you back in the temple by dawn."

"Oboy," said Mr. Gunfer.

Gen said slowly, "But we will reach the boats long before dawn." Staring puzzled at Ba Tu she said, "We will, won't we?"

Ba Tu turned to Chi Ti. "Tell them."

Chi Ti, still breathless, said, "You are surrounded!" He pointed to the north, to the east, west and south. "They make a circle. In the morning, when light comes—" With his hands he drew a circle in the air and then brought his palms together with a loud slap. To Ba Tu he said in Burmese, "I'm going, Ba Tu—no gold watch is enough for this. I met Bo Gale and he will not return either. It will be bad, very bad, to be found with these Ingalei and Ameiyikan."

The two of them moved away, arguing and gesturing. Gen looked at the others and said, "Chi Ti is too frightened to stay."

"He's deserting us?"

She nodded. "The other one, too."

Miss Thorald said, "How can he think we're surrounded? Just see how clear the road looks."

Lady Waring nodded. "We should go at once, quickly—tell him, Gen."

Chi Ti had slipped away in the darkness; Ba Tu turned back to them and Gen said softly, "He has gone?" When he nodded she asked, "And you, Ba Tu, will you go, too?"

He shook his head. "I have good fate—*kuthokan kaunde,*" he said with a faint smile. "You know if the gale of kan blows, a mountain of rock will be blown away. You know also our proverb, When circumstances are favorable water will flow uphill. It does not feel my time to die but we must make water flow uphill, Gen!"

"Yes," she said.

"How far away are they?" asked Lady Waring. "I don't understand how they could have surrounded us so soon."

"Look," said Ba Tu, pointing.

Far away to the south, where the woods curved in to meet the road, and the road vanished from sight behind them, the rooks that had nested in the trees at sunset were suddenly rising in a noisy flock to circle and fly away.

"There are men there," said Ba Tu quietly. "It is men who disturb them."

"Men from the jeeps?"

"I think," said Mrs. Caswell in a clear low voice, "that we must sit and be quiet for a minute, very quiet, while we think what to do. This is upsetting and confusing, and panic so often leads to rashness."

A faint breeze stirred the leaves above them and a bright disk of light fell on Ba Tu's face; he looked surprised. "Yes," he said, and obligingly joined them on the ground in the space they occupied between forest and field, darkness and moonlight.

And that is true, thought Gen, responding to such practicality, *I can learn much from this Mrs. Caswell who for so long concealed her true self.* "Now tell us, Ba Tu," she said. "If the jeeps carried soldiers to wait ahead of us, what else did Chi Ti tell you?"

He nodded. "The colonel guessed you would head south, he piled men into jeeps to get ahead of us very fast. Chi Ti said also men camp behind in the woods now, with spaces between them. A circle is being made."

They were silent until Baharian said softly, "To be tightened at some appointed hour. You know the area, Ba Tu, and you have experience, being a—a dacoit—is there hope for us?"

Gen did not wait for a reply. She said flatly, "We need guns."

Baharian said dryly, "Preferably loaded."

"But guns," repeated Gen firmly.

"They would certainly help," said Baharian, "but we have no guns."

"You can shoot?" asked Ba Tu.

Baharian nodded.

"Actually I can too," said Mr. Gunfer, and when they looked at him in surprise he said indignantly, "Did you think me 4-F in the war? I never saw action but I can assure you I went through basic training and have a sharpshooter's medal to prove it."

"I am not unacquainted with rifles myself," added Lady Waring, "having shot partridge frequently in more fashionable, bloodthirsty eras."

Eagerly Gen said, "Ba Tu, you remember the game of Enemy Spies we used to play when we were young, before you went away? Do you? Let's try for guns, the two of us! Remember how we hid and hunted each other like in war, and took turns being Bama and Japan?"

"Sade yanou, yes I remember, and you were best of all, we never found you. But this is no game, Zen."

"True," she said hotly, "but it is no game the colonel plays, they will begin coming and not miss a rock or a tree. Now is the

171

time to be bold and make water run uphill, Ba Tu, while the soldiers are careless."

"How many soldiers does the colonel have?" asked U Ba Sein.

Ba Tu shrugged. "Chi Ti said maybe forty-five, Ko Thein said forty."

U Ba Sein said softly, "That surely leaves many spaces—many gaps—in a circle . . . A dozen men in the jeeps, perhaps, the rest divided . . . not so many, after all."

Gen gave him an interested glance; she was sure that he was telling them something in his gentle way. How she knew this she couldn't explain but it had become apparent to her that at certain moments he guided their talk in directions that surprised them all. "See?" she said to Ba Tu. "We *must* try. You remember the tricks we used?"

"You have your slingshot?" he asked, and when she nodded he grinned, remembering. "Okay, let's try . . . we go!"

Lady Waring said sharply, "Don't take any chances!"

Baharian said, "I feel I should go, too, and help . . ."

"Bull in a tea shop," snorted Mr. Gunfer.

Mrs. Caswell whispered, "I'll pray for you, oh how I will pray for you!"

Ba Tu handed his empty rifle to Mr. Gunfer, saying, "It speaks even without bullets." Gen brought out her slingshot and checked her pocket for the stones she'd gathered when she was still with U Hamlin, and found that she much preferred action to waiting to be caged again, which brought to her the discovery of still another genevieve. Grasping Ba Tu's hand she crept with him back into the opaque darkness of the bamboo grove.

When they emerged from it they could see shapes and shades again but this meant they could be seen more clearly, too: much

172

care had to be taken, and because Ba Tu knew these woods she surrendered the lead to him, and followed. Tense as she might be at this moment she could feel the child in her responding and remembering: she adopted the same noiseless glide that Ba Tu used as he moved from one tree to the next and stopped to listen. They moved so slowly and so softly that no birds took flight, and had ventured perhaps half a mile when Ba Tu held up a hand.

Softly into her ear he breathed the words, "Ahead—*mi.*"

Peering over his shoulder she saw the glow of a fire between the trees ahead of them. "Campfire?" she whispered back.

He nodded. *"Shinde."*

They dropped to the ground, flat on their stomachs, and to reconnoiter slithered through the grass and over the earth like snakes, like swimmers. Reaching a sturdy oak they stood and peered around it at what lay beyond.

Ba Tu whispered, "I see three men."

"I see three rifles," she whispered back. "Ba Tu, you remember Chan Tu and the toddy palms?"

He chuckled. "I remember, Zen. You or me?"

In the dusky light she held up her slingshot. "I'll climb the tree, you wait below in case I miss. Be careful!"

Returning to hands and knees they crept closer, parting company in a dense growth of bamboo. Gen chose her tree carefully. Gripping the slingshot between her teeth she grasped the column of bamboo and shinnied upward, wincing when her bare knees drew blood from a sharp culm. Near the top she curled one leg around the neighboring bamboo and one arm around the column she occupied, and studied the situation below.

The three soldiers sat at their small fire warming themselves, two of them smoking cheroots, the other hugging his knees and grinning. They sat companionably, talking and laughing softly, their rifles on the ground beside them. Gen thought sternly, *Colonel Wang is not going to win his war with soldiers like these, obviously they cannot even wait an hour or two without building a fire and taking it easy.* Colonel Wang's loss, however, was her gain, and checking the stability of her position, which was precarious, she reached for her slingshot and three of her largest pebbles. Two stones went into her mouth, one was inserted into her slingshot. Again testing her foothold—it would not do to slip even an inch at such an important moment—she took aim at one of the heads below and fired off her stone. As the first left her slingshot and flew through the night a second was already on its way, and then a third. She lingered only long enough to see the first man fall flat, the second one reel and collapse, and then she began her drop to the ground sixteen feet below.

Ba Tu was struggling with the third man, whose temple had only been grazed. Gen, snatching up a fallen stick of bamboo, ran to help and this third man collapsed with an astonished look on his face. Turning to Ba Tu she grinned. "Oh Ba Tu, this has been *good. Akhu?*"

"*Akhu,*" he said, and snatching up the three rifles they fled, crashing through the underbrush in the opposite direction from which they'd come, then dropping to the ground and creeping back to the south, covering their tracks as they went.

15

"OH THANK HEAVEN," gasped Mrs. Caswell as they came out of the forest.

"Rifles?" gasped Baharian, seeing them. "Dear God I begin to hope we may yet survive this wild and suicidal flight into the night." Handed one by Gen he examined it and said, "And loaded, too? Good God! Where—how on earth—did you get these?"

Ba Tu said, "We found three soldiers in the wood and Zen knocked them out with her slingshot."

"With a *slingshot?*"

Gen said briskly, "Oh yes, for during the war it was the only way to kill food—rats and lizards and snakes, you know. One learns to aim very well when hungry enough. We go now, Ba Tu?"

"And we never knew," said Mrs. Caswell admiringly.

"We go."

Baharian received a rifle, Mr. Gunfer and Lady Waring were given theirs and in return Ba Tu retrieved his empty one. In a low voice he said, "We hurry along the edge of the woods now —quickly, please, and very softly—for one of the soldiers saw us, and when he opens his eyes again—"

"Say no more," said Mr. Gunfer, helping Lady Waring to her feet. "This suspense, this suspense—! Let's *go.*"

Ba Tu had uncoiled the rope and they fell in behind him, grasping the rope only loosely now, walking closer together as they left behind the moonlight and the view of fields. These were deep woods they entered, not the densely packed stems of the bamboo groves but scrub, flame trees and palms. Occasionally they stopped while Ba Tu listened carefully to the sounds of the forest, the cries of birds, the rustling of leaves; it began to seem possible that while soldiers waited behind them for a signal to move in, and soldiers were encamped a mile or two ahead, none of them were advancing as yet to corner them.

They had not slept for thirty hours, and the scarcity of food for eight days had depleted them. Nor had any of them, with the exception of Baharian, done much walking since captivity, so that each could admit to weariness, but not openly, since it was unaffordable with their lives in danger and survival uncertain. Nevertheless Lady Waring stumbled several times and against her protests Baharian walked beside her and supported her with his arm.

Sometimes the trees thinned as they turned briefly to the west and they caught glimpses of the fields they'd looked upon earlier, and saw the half-moon riding high in the dark sky. For the most part they trudged in a sober line, eyes on the ground lest they trip, stumble into a hole or run into a tree.

Ba Tu stopped at last. Gathering them into a circle he said,

"Now we must choose. We are very near to a good place to hide for a few hours, or we can go on and risk running into the jeep soldiers. It is true we have guns now and ammunition but it is very dark."

"What sort of hiding place?"

"A piece of earth in the deep woods with low walls around it, once a pagoda maybe." He shrugged. "Only walls are left—knee-high—but one can lie behind them and see and listen."

Gen said, "I choose to stop. To run into soldiers in the dark—"

Mr. Gunfer said, "But in the dark, if we're lucky, we could slip past them. If, as U Ba Sein pointed out, the soldiers are split up, how many can there be ahead?"

"Yes," said Miss Thorald, "and surely to try and pass them in daylight will be worse."

"On the other hand," said Lady Waring coldly, "I have not the *slightest* interest in being captured again and shot. If we run into soldiers in this stygian darkness we'd not have a chance in the world."

Baharian said, "If we can see them better in the daylight, they would see us better, too."

Mrs. Caswell pointed to Ba Tu. "You decide," she said.

"Ssh, not so loud," he counseled. "Okay, I decide. I take you to this hiding place and you wait while I am—what is word, spy? scout? and go ahead to see if I can learn just where they wait, and how many."

"Me too?" asked Gen eagerly.

He shook his head. "No, Zen. They would not capture me if I'm seen, for I carry with me a red arm band to wear, this is how I got through to you yesterday. If they stop me no harm will be done, but you are Ameiyikan."

177

"Compromise," said Baharian, nodding. "All right, let's try your hiding place while you reconnoiter."

"You will return?" Gen asked somewhat anxiously.

"I will return," Ba Tu said gravely.

Five minutes of walking took them into and through another thick grove of bamboo and then the bamboo thinned, brought to a stop by the ruin of a wall that kept the jungle of trees at bay. As Ba Tu had pointed out, the remaining walls were sufficient to hide behind, and if he did not add the words *and to shoot from behind,* this was implicit. Reminding them that soldiers were not far away now he went off to reconnoiter, leaving Baharian sprawled on the earth, his rifle resting on the south wall and his hand on the trigger while Mr. Gunfer guarded the north wall and Lady Waring chose to sit on a pile of fallen bricks in the center, her rifle across her lap. Mrs. Caswell and Miss Thorald had slumped with their backs against a wall. Gen busied herself in the rubble, feeling for stones of the right size to fit her slingshot, and then she sat down next to U Ba Sein to wait.

No one spoke. The minutes passed and then an hour. When Baharian shifted his position small pieces of rubble rearranged themselves, making sound. It was dark, and Gen could see only the shapes of them all but in her mind's eye she could see the details of each one and she thought, *We have become almost a family; eight days ago these people were strangers to me, I liked none of them, how did this happen?* And she said a little prayer to an uncertain God that Ba Tu would not be caught but would return to them safely, and that none of them would be captured again and shot.

It was after three o'clock in the morning when a cuckoo raucously shouted nearby; there was a stirring of branches and Gen called to Baharian in a low voice, "Don't shoot, it's Ba Tu."

He slipped noiselessly in among them and they surrounded

him. "It is *khette*—difficult—the soldiers built no fires, they were hard to find."

"How many are there?" whispered Baharian.

"I think six were in each jeep, maybe eight . . . in the dark I could not count foreheads, only listen to them talk. They form a line, three or four men, then inside of shouting distance three or four other men, with five soldiers guarding the jeeps, which are on the road. Ame, they seem very confident, and why not? I heard, I listened, at dawn they move in."

"Dawn," repeated Lady Waring.

Ba Tu nodded. "So at first light—very soon," he said, "we will go. Before dawn, before they move, but we must have enough light—just enough—to see them, this I tell you, this I know."

"More waiting," sighed Mr. Gunfer.

"Until we can see the shapes of each other," said Ba Tu, "because this will be the most dangerous move of all."

They returned to their established places and sat down again, but Ba Tu followed Gen to sit beside her. "Zen," he whispered, "I must speak with you."

"Ba Tu, I am here."

"Yes . . . Zen, I have thought much about this since seeing you again. Zen, if we get free—if your friends get through— come back with me to Theingyu!"

"Back?" she said, puzzled.

He nodded. "Already I have enough to buy twenty acres of land, I could go back tomorrow—even today—and not be a dacoit anymore. We could go together, Zen, you know Ma Nu would welcome you to our house. I will build a new compound for us all to share; you are already a daughter to her, Zen; if we marry it would make her glad. And me, too," he added simply.

She was touched; she said with feeling, "Don't tempt me, Ba

179

Tu, I would so love to say yes—to go back to Theingyu and to see everything that's familiar, and be a part of your family, and feel protected again. But I can't." Tears rose in her eyes as she thought of the words she'd spoken, and of the safeness she would feel.

"Then why, Zen, because your father told you to go to America?"

"No," she said softly. "No, my father made his choice and it was not—to me—a good choice that he made. I see now that it separates me from him so I needn't obey his wishes, but he chose what looked easy and this I will not do. It would be too easy to go back, Ba Tu."

"Zen, it will be very strange and different in America, and in Theingyu you have been loved."

She shivered. "I know this and it frightens me. I know it will be hard; there will be many people in America, many automobiles, and girls in ruffles and curls, and the streets will be paved and the cities big, and there'll be no village well for gossip, no pongyis at dawn, no flaming sunsets, no pagodas." She sighed. "But I will carry it all with me, Ba Tu—always. And you as well, and Ma Nu . . ."

"And Zawgwi," he said, feeling her pain and wanting to ease it.

She smiled at him through her tears. "You're a good person, Ba Tu, it's just that I have to see for myself, have to find out what it's like, and who I am in America and what I can be. If I go back to Theingyu I'll never learn this."

"It's not because I'm a dacoit?"

She touched his hand in response. "Oh no, Ba Tu, never."

"Is it the Ingalei you walked with?"

She shook her head. "Not that either, and in any case I'll never see him again. No it feels—very simply—my kan."

180

"Then I won't make it harder for you, Zen, but—it *was* fun stealing rifles, wasn't it? Just as it used to be?"

"It was, Ba Tu, it was," she told him gravely.

He nodded. "And now I can see—just a little—your eyes and nose and mouth, which means it is time to go. Keep your slingshot ready, Zen." He rose and went from one to the other, whispering to them, and they, too, rose.

The rope was merely carried now, wrapped snugly around Ba Tu's waist, for even though the moon was still in the sky and sunrise an hour distant the shapes of trees were slowly emerging out of the darkness. They moved slowly, almost on tiptoe, because each step took them nearer to the soldiers who encircled the forest and were poised to entrap them at dawn. Ba Tu led, with Baharian and his loaded rifle close behind him; the others followed, with Lady Waring placed in the center behind U Ba Sein and their third rifle in the hands of Mr. Gunfer, who brought up the rear. With the first light of day beginning to gray the sky, detail was added to their vague shapes and Gen saw what a tattered group they had become during the night, and how different they looked. Lady Waring's silk skirt was in shreds, her hair in wisps, and with a rifle slung across her shoulder she looked a brigand herself. Ahead of Gen a variety of palm leaves appeared to have dropped into Baharian's hair and taken root, while Miss Thorald's right cheek held a long smear of dirt. All of them were colored by dust, scratched by thorns, thirsty and cold and hungry.

They had negotiated a mile when Ba Tu stopped; he stood very still, his face puzzled in the gray light. "Listen," he said.

They heard it, too, now: a sound of firing ahead, a sudden volley of shots followed by silence and then a few sporadic exchanges and silence again.

181

"What is it?" asked Lady Waring, her voice loud and startling after so many hours of whispering.

"Fighting," said Ba Tu. "This may be our chance—let's go! Hurry!"

They came out of the woods not far from the road, but the road was obscured by a rise in the ground and the shooting came from the road. Gen said, "We've got to know what's happening." Dropping to the ground she crept cautiously toward the top of the hillock and the others followed in a ragged line until they all lay flat on their stomachs peering over the crest at the scene below.

It was a scene of confusion that needed time to sort out. The encircling Red Flag men had set up a roadblock with the two jeeps that had passed them in the night and they occupied the center of the dusty road, each identifiable by the shred of red cloth tied to its antenna. Three jeeps driving north had met the roadblock and had obviously been fired upon: from each of these jeeps—empty now—fluttered a Burmese flag.

"Government jeeps," Gen said in astonishment. "Those are government jeeps!"

"And captured," said Baharian grimly.

The men who had occupied the three government jeeps stood in the middle of the road surrounded by half a dozen soldiers wearing red arm bands, and it became clear that the thought of appropriating three precious jeeps had completely distracted the Red Flag soldiers from their assignment to capture the foreigners again.

It could be seen, too, that the government soldiers, a dozen in number, were weaponless; they held their hands high in surrender, and seeing this stirred anger in Gen, knowing now what capture meant.

And then she saw the sweater. It so astonished her that she

182

cried out, "But one of them wears my father's sweater—the black-and-white sweater my mother knitted for him! Look!" She pointed.

Quickly Mr. Gunfer pushed down her pointing hand. "Careful!"

But Gen was staring hard at the figure in her father's sweater. "It is," she whispered. "It is, I can't believe it but it *is,*" and to the others she gasped, "It's U Hamlin—he's here, it's my friend U Hamlin!" The wonder of it filled her: that he was still in the country, not even in Rangoon but *here,* with government soldiers, and was it possible—she dared not think so but was it not possible that having seen her captured he had come back to help free her?

The surge of warmth and pleasure at such a thought was followed by the horror of his predicament down on the road. She said to the others, "I think he's brought those government soldiers—guided them here—to rescue us, for why else would they be here in insurgent coun :y?"

"But who's Oohamlin?" asked Mr. Gunfer.

Gen turned and looked into U Ba Sein's face. "We must help them."

U Ba Sein nodded. "But of course."

To Ba Tu she said, "You met him. He mustn't be abandoned —somehow we must help him . . . and we have rifles now."

"And so have they," said U Ba Sein.

"I don't see them," she told him in a worried voice.

"On the ground, they've flung them to the earth."

She gave U Ba Sein a quick glance because she could see no rifles but if he said they were there she believed him. "Then what can we do?"

Ba Tu said slowly, "We have only three guns, it is not enough for so many. But if they could learn somehow we are here they could pick up their guns—if they truly have guns—and help. But I don't know how we could warn them we are here without Colonel Wang's men knowing we are here, too."

A smile spread over Gen's face. "I know how," she said. "Are we near enough to them, Ba Tu? Are we close enough to run down the hill with our rifles?"

Ba Tu nodded. "If there is a way to tell them, yes."

"I certainly can't run," said Lady Waring.

"Never mind, follow and cover us."

"But what is it you can do?" asked Mrs. Caswell.

Gen looked at U Ba Sein and smiled. "This," she said, and knowing that Hamlin would remember she opened her mouth wide and flinging back her head there came from her throat the wild, despairing, haunting and dirgelike cry of a ghost such as she had brought forth when she was with U Hamlin at the pagoda and with which she had frightened Chi Ti away from her money. Beside her Mrs. Caswell shuddered, and Ba Tu covered his ears. The piercing wail, coming as it did with the peacefulness of dawn hanging over them, brought confusion to the Red Flag soldiers and stirred even the birds, who took flight from the trees with a beating of wings. She saw U Hamlin whirl, look toward the hill and turn to speak to his companions. Rifles were snatched from the earth, and as Gen and Ba Tu led the way down the hill toward the road, Colonel Wang's men turned back to their prisoners to face a dozen rifles pointed at them. Now it was Red Flag rifles that were dropped to the ground, and six pairs of red-banded arms that were lifted in surrender.

And Gen, beaming as she crossed the road to Hamlin, extended one hand and said shyly, "U Hamlin, I am surprised and happy to see you again."

He laughed, and ignoring such formality he grasped her by

the waist and swept her into the air; returning her to earth he said, "Thank God you're safe—and by George, there's Mr. Like-his-Father, too!" And Hamlin, who had crept and crawled and stolen rides on ox carts to get help, who had been hidden by farmers and conveyed at last to Magwe in a truck driven by a chap who sang "Chattanooga Choo-Choo" all the way, now knew a little more of Gen's country, enough to say to Ba Tu, *"Htamin sa pibila?"*

Ba Tu shook his head, grinning, while Hamlin said, "I don't know who the rest of you are—"

"Save it," said Baharian. "Look at the sky."

"What about the sky?"

"It's nearly dawn, there'll be more soldiers coming at any minute," Gen told him, and while she described Colonel Wang's plans to him Ba Tu explained the danger in his own language to the AFPFL soldiers.

"Then we certainly can't allow these Red Flag chaps to go free and warn the others," Hamlin said. "That's a damn fine rope around your waist, Ba Tu, what about it?"

The rope was unwound, their sullen captives prodded into a group and roped together, and while they worked, the approaching dawn bleached the sky mother-of-pearl and in the east the first intimations of sun could be seen in a glow of saffron. By the time Colonel Wang's men lay ignominiously tied together at the side of the road a sliver of sun had already appeared in a burst of flame and gold.

With satisfaction Hamlin said, "And now we've five jeeps, not three. Time to go—hop in!"

But Ba Tu shook his head. "Not me," he said. "For me it is time to say goodbye to Zen and return to my friends. I go no further." From his pocket he brought out his red band of cloth and began to tie it around his arm.

Gen looked at him, knowing this had been inevitable, but still it was a wrenching moment for her and there were tears in her eyes at this final severing with Theingyu and her past. "I will miss you, Ba Tu," she told him solemnly, "and you have saved all our lives, which has to bring you much merit." She would have said more but a rifle was fired from the hill behind them, striking one of the jeeps with a metallic *ping!* "Here!" she cried, and fumbling in her shoulder bag she brought out her father's gold watch and thrust it into his hand.

"Hurry!" shouted Hamlin, and Gen and Ba Tu flew apart, he to take cover in a plunge among the trees, and Gen to leap into the jeep.

"Kaunde Kan, Mr. Like-his-Father," shouted Hamlin, and to his passengers, "Hold on now, we're going to drive like hell out of here and get you to the airport at Magwe!"

When Gen looked back Ba Tu had already vanished into the deeper woods, and a dozen Red Flag soldiers were racing down the hill to the road.

16

IT WAS EARLY AFTERNOON of the same day when they flew triumphantly into Rangoon, arriving in a patched-up troop transport that had been sent to Magwe to pick up government soldiers returning from the fighting around Mandalay. It was not a smooth flight, and for Gen it was her first, but crouched on the creaking floor of the plane she had reminded herself that a man from hell is not afraid of hot ashes, and she had invoked the Three Gems only once.

At Mangaladon Airport three men waited for them in the cavernous terminal building filled with dusty benches: Jordan from the American Embassy, Feathergale of the British Consulate and a representative of the Burmese government named Maung Yo. Feathergale, directing an *I-told-you-so* look at Lady Waring, spoke of how many people the insurgents had murdered lately, and Mr. Maung Yo made a brief speech congratulating them on having escaped execution. While it was being explained to Mrs. Caswell that the steamboat bearing her husband, Lady Waring's secretary and Culpepper would not reach Rangoon until Saturday, Jordan drew Hamlin aside.

Placing a hand on Gen's shoulder Hamlin propelled her out of the group with him.

Jordan said, "If you're Hamlin, you look younger than you sounded on the phone in Magwe."

"No doubt it was all that static," Hamlin said pleasantly. "You've been in touch with Washington?"

"Yes of course, I alerted them to your news at once. They'd about given you up for dead months ago, you know, so they want to see you as soon as possible. At the moment, getting out of here is on a strictly catch-as-catch-can basis but I've pulled strings and we've gotten you a seat on a plane for Bangkok tomorrow afternoon . . . Bangkok, Tokyo, San Francisco, et cetera . . ."

Hamlin considered this and shook his head. "Two seats."

Gen, only half listening, looked up startled.

"What do you mean 'two'?" said Jordan.

Hamlin smiled down at Gen. "This urchin here was giving me a great deal of help in my escape when she was captured. She goes with me."

Jordan looked at Gen with disapproval and at once she became aware of her ragged sneakers, outgrown dress and battered hat; her chin went up and she straightened her shoulders, which made Hamlin smile. "She's the one you went back for?"

Hamlin nodded. "Name of Perris, Zen Perris."

Gen said politely, "Actually it's Genevieve Ferris."

Jordan glanced down at the sheet of paper in his hand. "She's not on our list."

"No, the two of us were trying to reach the steamer when she was captured. We met over her father's—uh—burial, which makes her an orphan, Distressed Citizen and all that, and now she's on her way to an aunt in America."

Jordan said curtly, "Well, she'll have to wait her turn, Hamlin, we've only the one seat booked for you and that was damnably hard to get."

Hamlin smiled at him cheerfully. "Sorry."

"What do you mean 'sorry'?"

"Two seats."

"Why?"

"Because I've a fair knowledge of bureaucracy, and the girl could be here for weeks . . . months. Two seats. They've waited in Washington all this time, they can wait a little longer."

"Washington wants you *now*."

Hamlin only smiled. "Two seats."

"My God, you're a stubborn man." He looked broodingly at Gen. "Has she a passport?"

Gen dug into her shoulder bag and produced her precious passport and birth certificate.

Jordan, glancing over these, looked appalled. "My God, this passport expired years ago, it was issued in 1934. Do you realize the time it will take to apply for a new one?"

"There are such things as provisional passports, aren't there?" asked Hamlin. "Emergency passports, temporary passports?"

Jordan scowled at him. "Plus a seat on the plane? You drive a hard bargain, Hamlin. All I can promise is to take her papers along with me and see what can be done."

Gen, seeing him pocket her documents, reached out a hand to stop him. "Oh please—not without a receipt, they're all I have!"

Jordan looked at her, really seeing her now, and said with

189

some surprise, "I suppose that's true." Backing up to a bench he sat down, brought out pen and paper, copied data from both papers and handed her a receipt.

"Thank you," Gen said with dignity.

"Thank your friend instead," Jordan told her. "You'll have to come along with me now, Hamlin, there's a car waiting and we intend to keep you rather busy until plane time. Let's go."

"See you later," Hamlin told Gen, and lifted two fingers in a V sign.

Watching the two men walk out into the sunshine Gen realized in amazement that she might very well be on her way to America in only twenty-four hours and this produced a convulsion of emotions: the thought of still another venture into the unknown brought a wave of anxiety that bumped up hard against a thrill of excitement and anticipation. What she needed just now was the comforting presence of U Ba Sein, and she turned to find him.

"But where's U Ba Sein?" she asked, looking around the room, and when the others, talking, did not hear her she raised her voice in panic. "Where's U Ba Sein?"

Each of them, surprised, turned to look around the cavernous room.

Miss Thorald said, "He was here a minute ago."

Mrs. Caswell nodded vigorously. "He was standing between Mr. Gunfer and Lady Waring."

"But then he suddenly wasn't," said Lady Waring, puzzled. "Mr. Baharian, could you look in the lavatory?"

"But of course," said Baharian.

"What is it?" asked Lady Waring of Gen. "Is something wrong?"

"I may be leaving tomorrow, U Hamlin is trying to arrange it so I leave with him."

"Good heavens, so soon?" said Lady Waring. "Obviously sleep will have to be postponed, we must find you some decent clothes at once. Well, Mr. Baharian?"

Baharian shook his head. "He's not there."

"Then he's gone?" said Mrs. Caswell in surprise.

Feathergale glanced down at the list of names that Colonel Wang had so happily teletyped to them nine days earlier. "I see that your Mr. Ba Sein lives in Rangoon, do you know his address?"

"Yes of course we know *that,*" Gen told him impatiently.

"Then we'll find him there," said Lady Waring calmly, "for I want very much to see him myself. But we mustn't keep Mr. Feathergale waiting now, there's a great deal to be done before today ends." Seeing Gen's face she added gently, "It'll be all right, Gen."

"But without saying *goodbye* to us?"

"It'll be all right, we'll find him," repeated Lady Waring. "But now we must go . . . come along!"

Reluctantly Gen obeyed.

On the drive from the airport to the Strand Hotel Gen found that very little had changed in the city since she had left it five years ago. The great Schwedagon still soared toward heaven, puncturing the blue sky with its *stupas,* but the roads had not been repaved and were full of holes, and glancing into side streets and alleys she saw piles of refuse still being quarreled over by dogs. Rangoon had not yet recovered from a war that had left it devastated.

Lady Waring, on the other hand, found its Britishness refreshing after nearly losing her life in a remote temple on the Irrawaddy. She did not overlook the signs of deterioration everywhere, and no human being could possibly ignore the glittering spires of the Schwedagon but it was restful to her to see the reassuringly familiar British colonial architecture that by its very solidity and lack of imagination was an anodyne to the uncertainties they had recently endured. If her energies had been dangerously sapped during their escape she felt herself reviving now; she was, after all, known at the Strand Hotel, where she had spent the weeks before her departure on the steamer north, and both a room and fresh clothes waited for her. Therefore when they reached the hotel she did not walk into the lobby, she swept into it with all the prestige of a Lady Waring, and even went so far as to firmly take charge of them all. To Feathergale she said loftily, "I shall pay a call on you in—shall we say three hours? I want first to find this child some clothes for her trip, after which I wish to speak with you alone."

"Lady Waring," he stammered, "surely you're not thinking—surely you must realize that it could be months before it will be safe to—to—"

"—return to Upper Burma?" She smiled at him. "I will not be attempting it again, Mr. Feathergale, I will be returning to England as soon as Mr. Moreland reaches Rangoon and passage aboard ship can be arranged. No, it's something else I wish to speak about, thank you."

With a look of infinite relief Mr. Feathergale said, "Shall we say four o'clock, then?" When she nodded he added in a kindly voice, "Your best choice for clothes would be the black market you'll find behind the bazaar at this address." He scribbled directions on a card. "Until four, then."

Puzzled, Gen said, "I don't understand, Lady Waring, you're not going back to look for Eric's grave?"

Lady Waring shook her head. "No, my dear, I've two daughters in England—if it's not too late, that is—but perhaps only Mr. Ba Sein would understand."

"How soon can we visit U Ba Sein?" asked Gen.

"The bazaar first," Lady Waring said firmly. "I hear the water supply in Rangoon was cut off yesterday by the insurgents but is now in sufficient supply. We can only hope it remains so for a few hours longer because it seems most improvident to bathe and dress again in clothes you've worn for a week. I cannot help but have noticed," she added pointedly, "that Mr. Feathergale tried not to sit too near us in the car that brought us from the airport."

But even the black market bazaar held limited possibilities for Gen. They all went, except for Mr. Gunfer, who had heard that a freighter was leaving in the morning for Ceylon and had high hopes of booking passage on it. Miss Thorald and Mrs. Caswell bought longyis to wear until the steamer brought their clothes, and Baharian found a shirt and silk trousers to wear while his own clothes were laundered. What they found for Gen was a school uniform: a green wool pleated skirt with a white middy blouse and green tie. This was disappointing but she found solace in a pair of black pumps, her first pair of silk stockings and a tube of actual Tangee lipstick ("for lips men love and love to kiss"), and before they returned to the hotel Lady Waring added to Gen's wardrobe a quilted coat from China to protect her against January in America.

They found Mr. Gunfer in the hotel's bar. "Leaving in the morning," he told them, brandishing a ticket. His glance moved to Miss Thorald and Baharian, who had returned holding hands, and he said peevishly, "Are they going to be married, do you think?"

"There have been stranger couples," pointed out Lady Waring, "and after being closeted in a Burmese temple for eight days they must certainly know each other's faults. Actually Baharian would make a splendid father, and I rather think Miss

Thorald a good mother. Certainly she will make a crusade out of changing"—a faint smile played over Lady Waring's lips—"of changing her kan."

"Kan?" said Gunfer, with a sharp glance at her.

"I'm sure you heard me clearly. You continue staring at them, Mr. Gunfer, are you jealous of Baharian?"

Mr. Gunfer opened his mouth, closed it, was silent a moment and said curtly, "I might be."

Lady Waring smiled and patted him on the wrist. "Human after all. How old are you, Mr. Gunfer?"

"Thirty-eight," he said crossly.

Lady Waring shook her head. "For heaven's sake, Mr. Gunfer, you look and act fifty. Go back to your United States and act your age, you no longer have to eat beans and stale bread. Be a capitalist!"

"Never!" cried Mr. Gunfer.

"Then be a happy socialist."

"You are impertinent, Lady Waring!"

"They say we always see our faults in others," she told him blandly, and with a glance at the clock, "Oh dear, I shall be very late for Mr. Feathergale if I don't rush."

Gen, waiting in her hotel room for dinner, was drawn to the window to watch the sun slip behind the trees, leaving the sky suffused with changing shades of raspberry and lemon that slowly dimmed to a pale mauve. She was glad to be alone for these few minutes, and although she thought of many things she was most of all remembering a morning when she had asked U Ba Sein if there were thamma devas in America.

Very politely he had said no.

"But why, U Ba Sein?"

"Their ancient peoples know of thamma devas," he had told

her, "although they may call them by other names. And their prophets know of them, too, but no one listens to prophets."

"Then it will be very strange in America, U Ba Sein."

"Ah, but you will carry your thamma deva *inside* of you, Zen," he had said, "and if you listen—if you learn to listen—it will always be there for you."

She was listening for it now but all she could hear was the chatter of a gecko in the wall, and she had turned her thoughts to other matters when she became aware that she was not alone.

"You didn't hear my knock," said Lady Waring.

They looked at each other uncertainly, as people do when seen in different clothes and different environments, for Gen was now scrubbed and groomed and Lady Waring wore a silk beige dress in which she looked elegant and expensive. "You're back from seeing Mr. Feathergale?"

Lady Waring nodded and said curiously, "What were you thinking of when I walked in, Gen?"

"Of all that I've loved here," Gen said softly. "Not the terrible war years but the others—how it was before the war in Maymyo, in the hills, with my mother and father alive and flowers everywhere . . . And I was thinking of Theingyu too, and the monastery just beyond the village with its teak walls and the glitter and gilt of the Buddha images, and the river flowing past, and how wherever one looks there's the glimpse of a pagoda. Suvannaphumi . . . did you know that's what Burma was called in the ancient days? It means the Golden Land."

To hear the child talk so openly was a gift in itself, and Lady Waring smiled. "There are people who insist that we're made of bone and flesh and muscle but I say instead that we're made of memories. Cherish them but don't live in them, Gen, or they'll destroy all the bridges to your future."

195

Gen looked at her with interest. "Is that why you're going back to England?"

"I think," said Lady Waring, "that if there is such a thing as a spirit hovering over its burial place, then Eric must be very happy to find himself in your Suvannaphumi rather than in a cold stone crypt in England. Yes, I believe I've let go of my grief and pain, Gen. I discover—and I have U Ba Sein to thank for it—that it's time I live for the living. Which is why I want you to have these," she said, handing her a small chamois pouch.

Puzzled, Gen took the pouch, loosened its strings and opened it. "Your *pearls?*" she gasped.

"I don't like worrying about people," Lady Waring told her crossly, "and I should worry a great deal about you going off to heaven knows what with no money. I know nothing of that aunt of yours or her situation—nor do you—but these ought to see you through college, four years of it, if that's what you want. They're certainly valuable enough to do *something,*" she said firmly. "It's what I discussed with Mr. Feathergale, and we drew up papers for the Customs people, stating they're a gift from me to you."

Without a word Gen went to her and put her arms around her, incapable of expressing what she felt but knowing that Lady Waring, too, was incapable of this, which made words unnecessary. They stood like this for a long and deeply felt moment until Lady Waring released her, saying gently, "It's time we meet the others for dinner but there's one more thing I want to say."

Gen looked at her and waited.

"I will say it now," she told her, "because I plan to have a luxurious sleep in a real bed as soon as dinner is behind us, and

196

in the morning we visit U Ba Sein. You have not had a mother lately to tell you this, Gen, but I want you to know that despite your concern you *will* have breasts. Believe me."

On this congenial note they went down to dinner.

17

IN THE MORNING, quite early, Gen and Lady Waring climbed into an ancient DeSoto taxi outside the hotel and after Gen had given the driver the address, and after Lady Waring had haggled over the price, which she had learned was a necessity during her long wait to go north, they set out with a shudder and a clanging of gears for the Jubaliho Theater at number 16 Jubaliho Street.

The air was cool and full of fragrant spicy smells with traces of wood smoke. The taxi threaded its way among trishaws and bicycles, past open-air cafés, shops, markets and a number of massive government buildings. They did not speak; the old car was noisy but it was also to be a day of partings, which gave Lady Waring a feeling of uncomfortable solemnity. One parting had already taken place: they had been the only two people breakfasting early enough to see Mr. Gunfer leave, and Lady

Waring was still trying to forgive herself for her attack of sentiment at his departure: she had actually embraced and kissed him, which had startled them both.

Their taxi driver spoke. "Jubaliho Street," he said, pointing, as they turned off a broad avenue into a narrower road, and Gen leaned forward eagerly to watch.

On the corner stood a decaying mansion with pockmarked stucco and broken shutters, its yard crowded with squatter huts. A few tall palms lined the street with tops like ragged dust mops, and in every crevice between the buildings the basic jungle of the country erupted in greenery. At the next intersection the street changed into one of commerce, with layer upon layer of shops and signs and several British colonial buildings into which people and shops had poured. Only one vacant space could be seen on the street, like a tooth extraction that leaves a gap, and it was beside this that their taxi stopped. Gen looked out on a flat, rubble-filled square of land, empty except for a bookstall set up at the corner of the lot that was occupied by a man who sat behind its counter, hands folded patiently in his lap.

Puzzled, she said to the driver, "Why have you stopped? This can't be number 16."

He shrugged. Pointing a finger at the bookstall he announced that the printing shop beyond the bookstall was number seventeen, the lacquer factory behind them was number fifteen, and this was therefore number sixteen.

Gen said indignantly, "U Ba Sein wouldn't lie to us, there should be a theater here!"

"Wait for us," Lady Waring told the driver commandingly, and to Gen, "He's made a mistake, we'll ask."

They stepped out and approached the bookseller, who rose to greet them. "Two Ingalei! May I help?"

"Ameiyikan," Gen told him automatically. "We're looking for the marionette theater, the Jubaliho, at number 16."

Surprised, he said, "But there is no theater here, as you can see."

"Yes, one can see that," Gen said, "but it has to be somewhere here, we were given the address only a few days ago. Is it nearby?"

He thought about this. "I do not think so but Kau Reng will know—come," he said, and he led them across the road to a shop over which hung a sign announcing in both English and Burmese that it was the Pan Photo Studio. He shouted into a dark interior and his call produced a troop of small children, followed after an interval by a bent old man with a cane.

"Kau Reng, these two ladies look for a marionette theater called the Jubaliho."

The old man looked curiously at Lady Waring and Gen. "It's been a long time," he said. "The Jubaliho?" He thrust out his underlip and nodded. *"Takhau, hou'ke."*

"He says 'once, yes,' " translated Gen, puzzled, and to Kau Reng, "What do you mean, once?"

He stretched out a thin arm to indicate the field of rubble across the street. He said in English, "It stood *there,* very tall, very grand, like a pagoda. Ame, so many people came to see, and the shows?" His eyes brightened. "I saw them myself when I was a child—so high!"

"But where is it now?" asked Gen.

"Nowhere." He shrugged. "The puppetmaster died, it was torn down."

"But that's impossible," protested Gen.

The bookseller, listening, said, "Wait—I think I have a book. In a certain year the King himself, and the Queen, attended a

200

yokthe pwe and there is a program, a booklet, I know it is somewhere in my shop. Of much interest, surely!"

Gen would have preferred to leave, but an inertia born out of bewilderment and alarm was undermining her and so they followed the bookseller across the dusty road again to his bookstall, neither of them speaking or looking at each other, and patiently watched while the man thumbed through stacks of ragged magazines and then vanished among the shelves in the rear. When he returned he was triumphant.

"You wish for a souvenir? You can have it for ten kyat." He shoved aside a pile of books and placed his discovery on the counter in front of Gen and Lady Waring. It proved to be several bound sheets of yellowing newsprint with its first page displaying a tinted, fading rotogravure of a building. "There," he said, "this is your Jubaliho, it says so. And the story of it."

Reluctantly Gen feigned interest in the picture of a pagoda-shaped structure with a string of lights outlining it, but it was U Ba Sein she had come to find and her feelings of hurt and confusion were deepening. He had misled her, he'd lied to her, he had not been a puppetmaster after all, and the fact that he'd not even said goodbye sealed his betrayal.

"And here is the King and the Queen," said the bookseller proudly, turning to the second page.

"Yes, very attractive—thank you," murmured Lady Waring.

Gen said impatiently, "I can't read Burmese, there's no point in looking at this, I want to go, I want—"

She stopped in midsentence because Lady Waring had extended one finger to idly turn the page, and an eerie silence fell between them as they stared at the photograph of the man dominating the center of this last page.

Gen said in a small, frightened voice, "Who . . . Please, can you tell us what's written under this picture?"

The bookseller brought out a pair of glasses, placed them on his nose and peered at the photo. "Ah yes," he said warmly, "this was the man who began the theater, a very famous puppetmaster."

Lady Waring said sharply, "And where is he now? Where can we find him?"

The bookseller looked surprised. "It says—but of course you cannot read Burmese?—he died in 1920."

Gen closed her eyes, her heart beating very quickly, nearly suffocating her at his words, even as a part of her thought, *Yes, it would be like this, it would have to be.* She opened her eyes, which —to her astonishment—were filled with tears, and she said quietly, "And what was his name?"

"A most famous name," the bookseller told her. "He was U Ba Sein."

"Yes," she said, and drew a deep breath.

In a shaken voice Lady Waring said, "I think we will go now." And hastily dropping a ten-kyat note on the counter, and with a nod to the bookseller, she grasped Gen by the arm and led her away.

They climbed into the waiting taxi without speaking, and were driven back past the decaying mansion, the government buildings, the markets, the shops and open-air cafés, and of the two of them Gen was the happier for she felt at peace and touched by miracle.

Not until the taxi drew up to the hotel did Lady Waring turn and look at her. She said fiercely, "I do not think we will speak of this, we will tell the others that Mr. Ba Sein was not at home."

Gen looked at her with interest.

"It's too unsettling," she said. "What can I do but reject the impossible? It would be very pleasant, of course, to think that once in a while, once in a great while—" She shook her head. "I'm too much of the world to believe in such things."

"Yes," said Gen.

"Nevertheless, before we go inside, Gen Ferris, I will ask—" She bit her lip, hesitating.

"Yes?"

"Ask just once what you're thinking. *Now*. At this moment."

"I don't mind," Gen said softly. "I am thinking that U Ba Sein was everything he said he was, a puppetmaster, but a very strange and different sort of puppetmaster, because the puppets he guided and the strings he pulled—"

I have come this way to meet someone, U Ba Sein had told Baharian, and to Lady Waring he had said, *A puppetmaster is always busy—here and there.*

"There is no need to finish," said Lady Waring sharply. "Let's leave it at that, shall we?" And they went inside to join the others.

And so in the month of Pyatho, in the year 2494 of the Burmese Era, and in the year of Our Lord 1950, Gen—in the company of U Hamlin—left behind Burma and sixteen years of a not uneventful life. She carried with her a battered felt hat, a pearl necklace, certain memories to cherish, the puppet Zawgwi and an awareness of many new genevieves to be learned and explored.

In the several years that followed, a new Cynthia Gore novel was published and welcomed by its readers; it concerned a small group of people captured by dacoits and closeted in a jungle temple, its heroine a young woman with hair the color of ripe apricots.

Miss Thorald and Baharian were married in San Francisco and eventually, as children arrived, she became president of the

PTA, and a den mother, and no one ever heard again of a murderess named Lina Lerina.

Lady Waring wrote many letters to Gen from her cottage in Cornwall, where she distributed kindness among her neighbors, her daughters and her grandchildren. She did not return to Burma.

From Mrs. Caswell came postcards from Syria, and then from Egypt, where she continued to observe and to collect the pains and exultations of living.

And during those years Hamlin learned why he had been compelled to return to Badamyâ and to find Gen again.

From U Ba Sein nothing is heard but Gen often finds herself at the window on a clear moonlit night sending thoughts into the sky to a star too distant to be seen by the naked eye. U Hamlin, having seen what he saw at the pagoda, does not think her a fool.

ABOUT THE AUTHOR

Dorothy Gilman is the author of eight popular Mrs. Pollifax mysteries and several other well-received novels. She lives in Albuquerque.